DEAD TIDE

LEIGHANN DOBBS

1

Celeste Blackmoore felt a trill of excitement as she pushed open the door to *Rita's Eats*. She scanned the diner, her heart skipping just a little when her eyes found the small, elderly man sitting in the last booth. She made her way down the aisle and slid into the bench opposite him, the red naugahyde seat squeaking as she scooted across it.

"You have some news, Mr. Skinner?" Celeste raised an eyebrow at the man.

Reinhardt Skinner's eyes, magnified by the thick lenses of his round eyeglasses, glittered with excitement. He pushed his half eaten sandwich to the side and leaned across the table toward her.

"I may have found something very important in your journal," he said in a low voice.

Celeste's heartbeat picked up speed. She'd hired the historian to decipher a three hundred year old journal that had belonged to a distant relative of hers. The journal had been found in the attic of the family home she shared with her three sisters ... a home which had been the location of a deadly treasure hunt only months before. The journal had started the treasure hunt and, while Celeste's sisters thought the treasure was long gone, she held out a hope that there might be something worthwhile in the journal. The only problem was that it was in some sort of code, thus the need for Reinhardt Skinner.

"Oh? What?"

Skinner glanced around the diner. A bead of sweat formed on his forehead. He pulled a white linen handkerchief out of his pocket and swiped at his face.

"This may be the most important find of my career." He tugged at his red bow tie, pulling it out and loosening the top button of his crisp, white shirt.

"What did you find?" she persisted.

"Well, if what I think I have uncovered is true, this could be a find of historical importance." He gulped in a wheezy breath. "Not to mention financial significance."

"Go on." Celeste bit back her impatience, feeling a jolt of concern at the man's red face and labored breathing.

Skinner reached across the table putting his clammy hand on top of hers, his black eyes boring into her blue ones. She could feel the excitement rippling off him and her heart skittered in anticipation.

"Miss Blackmoore, it seems you might be sitting on top of Aghh—"

His eyes grew wide and he jerked his hand away to clutch at his chest. Celeste's heart leapt into her throat as she heard him make a sickening gurgling sound. His eyes bulged in their sockets and he slumped over sideways in the booth.

Celeste jumped out of her seat and ran to his side.

"Someone call nine-one-one!"

* * *

CELESTE WAS STILL ATTEMPTING CPR when the ambulance arrived even though Mr. Skinner was clearly beyond help. The EMT's took over and she collapsed into the booth.

"Well, well, well, if it isn't one of the Blackmoore's. You gals always seem to end up with a dead body on your hands."

Celeste felt her stomach sink at the grating voice. She turned to see Sheriff Overton standing in the doorway glaring at her. She cringed as he ambled toward her, his oversized belly protruding over his belt, a toothpick bobbing up and down in his mouth.

"What have we got?" The question was directed at the EMT, but Overton kept his beady eyes on Celeste.

"Looks like a heart attack," the EMT said as he started rolling the body away.

Overton watched him go then turned back to Celeste. "And you're right in the middle of it. Big surprise."

Celeste took a deep breath to squelch the spark of anger she felt. Overton had become sheriff in the seaside town of Noquitt, Maine five years ago—shortly after her mother had killed herself by jumping off a cliff into the ocean. Celeste had only been eighteen and had watched the investigation through anguished teenage eyes. She hadn't been impressed with him then and was even less so now. For some reason Overton seemed to have it in for her and her sisters and relished accusing them of almost every crime that happened in their small town.

"So tell me, why *are* you here?" Overton switched the toothpick from one side of his mouth to the other.

"I was meeting Mr. Skinner for lunch."

Overton's brows shot up. "Kind of old for you isn't he?"

Celeste suddenly became aware of the entire diner staring at her. She squirmed in her seat.

"We had hired him to validate some of our family heirlooms." She didn't need the whole town knowing they had a journal that might lead to treasure—or if Skinner was right, an important historical find.

Overton narrowed his eyes at her. "And that's why you were here with him?"

Celeste nodded. "He was telling me about … ummm … the items."

"And what were they?"

"I don't see how that's relevant. The man had a heart attack for crying out loud. He *was* pretty old."

Overton's face tightened and he wrote something in a notebook he had produced from the top pocket of his shirt.

"It appears that way, Ms. Blackmoore. But I have a feeling you're up to no good. We'll see what the medical examiner has to say—given the fact that you were just in my jail a few short months ago on murder charges I'm going to have to treat this as a possible homicide."

"What? You know those murder charges were trumped up by *you*!" Celeste rose from her seat, fists clenched at her side. "The real murderer was caught and my name was cleared."

Overton laughed and Celeste's cheeks flamed knowing she had played right into his hands letting him get a rise out of her.

"Well, be that as it may, I have a sneaking suspicion that any death that involves you Blackmoore girls has a lot more to it than meets the eye. I'd be willing to bet this isn't the last time I'll be questioning you," Overton said shoving the notebook in his pocket and turning in the direction of the front door.

Celeste stared after him, fighting the urge to stick her tongue out at his retreating back. As she watched him get into his cruiser in the parking lot, her thoughts turned to Reinhardt Skinner.

She hadn't known him well, but she was truly sorry that he was dead. Not only because she'd liked the old historian, but also because now, she was going to have a heck of a time figuring out what the "important find" was that he was trying to tell her about just before his badly timed death.

2

C eleste closed the thick oak door of her ocean front home and leaned against it with a sigh. The twenty-four room house had been in her family for three hundred years and it had a calming influence on her psyche. For some reason just walking through the door always seemed to wash away the stresses of the day. And today she needed that, especially with the way Reinhardt Skinner had died right in front of her.

"Mew."

Belladonna, the family cat, weaved figure eights between her ankles and Celeste bent down to pet her silky white fur.

"So, how was your day?"

Belladonna just stared at her with ice blue eyes and flicked her tail.

"Mine wasn't that great. I need a treat."

Celeste made her way down the front hall to the kitchen. Like many of the rooms in the house, the spacious kitchen had been an add-on built sometime in the mid-1800s. It still had the original dark mahogany, Victorian cabinets which were offset by white marble counters. Stainless steel appliances were a newer addition as was the island which had a sink in the center.

Celeste breezed past the island to a thick, wooden door on the far wall. The door led to the basement. Celeste felt a chill run up her spine as she approached it. She yanked it open, her nose wrinkling at the damp smell that greeted her.

The girls never went in the basement—it was dark and creepy and their mother had threatened them with severe punishment if they even thought about going down there when they were little. As far as Celeste was concerned, the threats were unnecessary. She'd been down there once and remembered a cavernous room with a dirt floor. A big brick well stood in the middle and spiders and other creepy crawlies skittered around in the corners. She'd had no desire to go down there when she was a little girl and even less of a desire to do so now.

It was, however, a great place to keep paper bags filled with the end of season garden tomatoes—the ones that you want to slowly ripen so that you can still have fresh tomatoes into the fall. They kept the bags three steps down where it was cool enough to do the trick, but not far enough down so they had to venture into the basement.

Celeste pushed the door open all the way and stood on the first step, bending down to reach the bag two steps below. Something brushed against her leg and her heart stopped … then started up again when she realized it was only Belladonna.

She grabbed the bag and was about to turn and rush into the safety of the kitchen when she noticed the cat was five steps down.

"Mew." Belladonna looked over her shoulder at Celeste and flicked her tail.

"Belladonna, get back up here." Celeste indicated the open door, but the cat just stared at her and took another step down.

Celeste's heart crunched. She didn't want the cat to get stuck in the basement. She made swooshing noises and waved her hand toward the door.

Belladonna sat down and licked her paw.

"Oh, for crying out loud." Celeste shoved the paper bag into the kitchen and tip toed down to the fourth step. She bent down to scoop up the cat, making the mistake of looking into the darkness that loomed below them.

Her heart froze when she saw a little wisp of vapor

at the bottom of the steps, swirling around as if it was beckoning to her. She blinked and it was gone. It might have just been her imagination, but she'd seen that type of vapor before and knew what it meant.

A ghost.

So far, all the ghosts she'd talked to had been friendly ones. Her grandmother and her spirit guide, Andrew. But they always appeared in warm, comforting places.

She had no idea if the basement ghost would be friendly or not … and she had no intention of sticking around to find out. Grabbing Belladonna she lurched up the steps, into the kitchen and slammed the door shut behind her.

"What the heck?"

Celeste jerked her head in the direction of the voice, dropped the cat on the floor and got into her most defensive karate position, her heart beating wildly in her chest.

"What is going on?" Her younger sister, Jolene stood in the kitchen, her chocolate brown curls matching her brows that were arched over ice-blue eyes.

Celeste relaxed.

"Oh, sorry. That basement always spooks me." She didn't want to get into the whole ghost thing with Jolene. Her sisters were just barely accepting the notion that she talked to their dead grandmother. She didn't know what they would think if she told them she was seeing other ghosts too.

"What are you doing home anyway?"

"I'm just doing some homework for my computer forensics course."

Jolene, the youngest of the four sisters, had graduated high school the previous year and floated around most of the summer trying to find herself. After doing some computer work that helped them clear their oldest sister from a bogus murder charge, she'd finally found her calling—computer forensics.

Now she was taking a course at the local college and starting a new career working for their other sister's boyfriend Jake, a former Noquitt cop, who had just hung up his shingle as a private investigator.

Thinking about it made Celeste smile. Jolene had only been fourteen when their mother died and she'd been hit pretty hard. The sisters had tried their best to get her through high school but she'd been a bit hard to handle. Even though it was mostly Morgan and Fiona that had done the "mothering" Celeste had done what she could and felt a glow of satisfaction that Jolene was finally on the right track.

"Did you meet with the historian?" Jolene's question interrupted Celeste's thoughts and she frowned.

"Yeah, but I have some bad news about that."

Celeste took the brown bag over to the kitchen island, grabbing a knife from the drawer on the way.

"Bad news?"

"Well good news *and* bad news, actually." Celeste reached into the bag and pulled out a bright red tomato the size of her fist.

"Give me the good news first." Jolene handed a small cutting board to Celeste who got to work slicing the tomato.

"Well, he said that he had made some progress figuring out the code in the journal."

Jolene's eyebrows shot up. "That's great."

Celeste nodded, still focused on the tomato. "Even better, he said that if his findings were correct it could have historical significance ... and be worth a lot of money."

"What could be bad about that?"

Celeste looked up from spreading the tomato slices out on a plate. "The bad part is that he dropped dead before he could tell me exactly what his findings were."

* * *

"WHAT DO YOU MEAN 'DROPPED DEAD'?" Jolene's ice-blue eyes widened.

Celeste shrugged. "I guess he had a heart attack. One minute he was sitting across from me in the booth and the next he was making gargling noises and keeling over."

"Oh, the poor guy."

"Yeah, he was a nice man." Celeste sprinkled sea salt on the tomato slices and pushed the plate toward Jolene. "Help yourself."

Jolene picked up a bright red slice and lifted it to her mouth. "So, we need to find someone else to decipher the journal then?"

"Why would we need to do that?" Celeste's oldest sister, Morgan, asked from the kitchen doorway where she leaned against the opening in her usual calm manner.

"Celeste just told me the guy we hired is dead," Jolene said.

"Who's dead?" Fiona appeared behind Morgan, her fiery red curls and tense stance matching her feisty personality.

"Reinhardt Skinner. I guess he had a heart attack." Celeste bit into a tomato slice, her mouth watering with the earthy, salty flavor.

"When did he die?" Fiona took a seat at the kitchen island and grabbed a slice of tomato.

"At lunch with Celeste," Jolene said.

"You were with him?" Morgan turned to Celeste.

"Yep."

"What happened?"

"Well, we were eating lunch and he grabbed his chest and keeled over. I tried to do CPR but it was really too late. The EMT's came and said there was nothing left to be done." Celeste frowned. "Oh, and Overton came."

"Oh, I bet he loved finding you with a dead body." Morgan stood on her tiptoes to reach up to the top shelf of one of the cabinets, her long, silky black pony tail swinging from side to side.

"Yeah. He made the usual snide remarks, but at least this time there were plenty of witnesses that can vouch that I didn't kill him."

"Because he wasn't murdered," Jolene added.

"Yeah, lucky for me he died of natural causes." Celeste bit into another tomato slice.

"Or unlucky for you," Jolene said, "because he did have some interesting news."

"Really?" Morgan turned from the cabinet with the homemade herbal tea bag she'd apparently been searching for.

"Yeah, I was just telling Jolene that he said he may have found something significant in the journal."

"Significant *and* worth a lot of money," Jolene added.

"Which is why she was asking if we need to get someone else," Celeste said.

"So there really is a treasure, then." Morgan sipped her steaming cup of tea.

"Well, he didn't actually say *treasure*, but he did use the words significant and valuable."

"Sounds like a treasure to me," Fiona said looking out the window toward the Atlantic Ocean. "And that means we might find ourselves fighting off pirates again."

Celeste shivered as she followed Fiona's gaze across Morgan's herb garden to their side yard, where the cliff sat eighty feet above the Atlantic Ocean … or the big gaping hole where the cliff once was.

Earlier in the summer, the journal had led them to an old treasure map which had started a hunt for a cache their ancestor, Isaiah Blackmoore, was rumored to have buried. Unfortunately, modern day pirates had tried to get to it first. What no one knew was Isaiah had booby trapped the site and when the pirates tried to take it, they blew off half the cliff—and themselves—in the process.

The modern day pirates had been a nasty bunch, killing at least one man, breaking into Celeste's home and even kidnapping Morgan to get her to reveal the location found on the map. Celeste cringed at the thought of having to deal with anyone like them again.

"But I thought the treasure was either blown into the ocean or dug up long ago," Jolene said.

Celeste shrugged. "Who knows? All I know is that Skinner said he made an important find and I want to know what it is."

The three sisters nodded their agreement.

"So what do we do now?"

"He must have had some notes," Fiona said.

"Right. And we need to get the copies of those journal pages we gave him and the poetry book," Morgan added.

"So we need to visit his office." Celeste picked up the last tomato slice and popped it in her mouth.

"I guess it's a good thing we didn't give him the original journal," Jolene said.

"Yeah, I would hate to think of that just sitting around in his office where anyone could take it." Morgan bobbed her tea bag up and down in her mug. "As it is, I feel a little nervous about him having the key book."

Celeste bit her lower lip. Isaiah Blackmoore's journal had been written in code. A certain type of code called a book cipher that required a second book in order to decipher it. The way it worked was that the words in the journal referred to certain passages in the second book, called the key, and those passages revealed the actual word in the message. They had given the key, a poetry book, to Skinner and they'd need it back if they had hopes of a new historian taking over the job. And the only way to get it back was to go to his office at the museum and take it.

"Okay, so who wants to go to the museum with me tomorrow?" Celeste asked.

"I will, if Fiona doesn't mind watching the shop in the morning." Morgan glanced at Fiona who nodded her assent. The two sisters had a store, *Sticks and Stones*, where they sold herbal remedies and crystal healing stones and jewelry.

"Okay, sounds like a plan," Celeste said.

"Great. I think the museum opens at eight, so if we leave here by seven thirty tomorrow morning we'll get there right when they open." Morgan looked at Celeste for confirmation, and her ice-blue eyes clouded over. "I think it would be smart to keep this to ourselves. I have a funny feeling that letting word get out about this important find could be very dangerous for us."

3

C eleste jumped out of bed the next morning just as the sun was starting to make its appearance. She pushed aside her sheer purple curtains and shoved open the wooden window, struggling against the ancient weights that held the window in place.

Her room was in one of the oldest parts of the house. The windows could use some modernizing, but she loved the other details of the room like the marble fireplace, glass doorknobs and wide pine floors.

The corners of her lips turned up in a smile as she leaned out the window taking a deep breath of sharp, salty sea air. Her room had a gorgeous view of the Atlantic Ocean and she'd been privileged to view decades of spectacular sunrises from it. Those sunrises always lifted her spirits, not that she really needed it—

Celeste was normally a very happy and positive person.

This morning, she was her usual upbeat self, except for one small thought that irritated her conscious like a piece of grit inside an oyster. She couldn't forget Morgan's warning the night before and how she'd said she had "a funny feeling" word getting out about the important find could be dangerous. Over the summer Celeste had come to recognize that Morgan's feelings usually turned out to be right and Celeste couldn't shake that dark foreboding she'd felt when she'd heard her warning.

She took another deep breath and made a conscious effort to push her worries aside. It promised to be a gorgeous day and she wanted to start it off right with a glass of wheat grass juice and herbs from the garden.

She ran her fingers through her short blonde hair, not really caring how she looked. There was no one here to see her except her sisters and she didn't really care about impressing people with her looks anyway. She pushed her feet into a pair of purple flip-flops and started toward the door.

"Mew." Belladonna stretched, her front legs elongated in front of her.

"Where did you come from?" Celeste frowned at the cat. She didn't remember letting Belladonna into her room the night before and the door was closed.

Then again, the cat seemed to have a way of appearing out of nowhere … especially when she wanted food, which was probably what she was after now. Celeste was always the first one up and the cat always knew just who to follow to get her breakfast.

Celeste opened the door and made her way to the kitchen with Belladonna trailing at her heels.

In the kitchen, she dumped some cat food into Belladonna's bowl, grabbed a pair of scissors from the drawer, and headed out the side door to the garden. Picking her way through the rows of herbs, she headed toward the far corner where her little patch of wheatgrass grew.

Although the sisters shared the garden space for whatever they wanted to grow, it was mostly home to Morgan's various herbs—her sister was a master herbalist and loved growing her own organic plants to use in the remedies she sold at *Sticks and Stones*. On her way to the wheat grass, Celeste passed a few herbs she recognized such as basil, echinacea, and chamomile. She also passed dozens of others for which she knew neither the names nor what remedies they were used in.

The garden was both aromatic and beautiful. Most of the herbs boasted gorgeous flowers, like the echinacea with its purple petals. Morgan had perfected her growing technique to extend the growing season for many of the plants and the garden was still flourishing, even in September.

Celeste stopped at the wheat grass which was neither aromatic nor beautiful, but made up for that with its many health benefits. As she bent to cut a handful, she saw Belladonna pawing at something a few rows over.

She squinted over at the cat and her heart froze when she recognized the purple spires of flowers. Monkshood. Wasn't that one of the plants Morgan said was toxic?

"Belladonna … shoo!" Celeste waved her arms, catching the cat's attention.

"Get away from there." Celeste jerked her head in the direction of the catnip two rows over. Belladonna took the hint, shaking her head then plodding off toward the catnip and proceeding to nibble.

Celeste grabbed a handful of wheatgrass and picked some parsley and mint for flavor then headed back to the kitchen.

She was feeding the wheat grass, parsley and mint into the juicer, along with some spinach, when Morgan appeared freshly showered and wearing black jeans, a white tee-shirt and black blazer.

Celeste looked down at her pajamas. "Do you think I'm underdressed for the museum?"

Morgan laughed. "Maybe a tad. I just figured if I

looked a little professional maybe they wouldn't mind us poking around in Skinner's files. I have to admit I'm a little worried about getting his notes. Do you think they'll just give them to us?"

"I was wondering about that myself. I'm not even sure how we will know which notes are about the journal, but all we can do is try."

"Yeah, I guess." Morgan grabbed a mug from the cabinet and set about making hot water for tea.

"Do you think we should ask them to recommend another historian while we are there?" Celeste asked as she settled into a chair at the kitchen island.

Morgan wrinkled her brow. "I'm not sure. We'd need someone who is really discreet. I don't want word getting ou—"

"Meoooow!" Celeste's heart jerked as she saw a white blur hurtle across the kitchen hitting the basement door and landing in a writhing pile.

"Belladonna! Are you okay?" Morgan rushed over to the cat who squirmed on her back, then flipped in the air twisting herself around before she landed.

The cat then proceeded to roll around on her back making mewling noises. Celeste was relieved to recognize this as the way she acted when she was high on catnip.

"What the heck?" Morgan's brows mashed together as she looked up at Celeste.

Celeste shrugged. "Catnip"

"Oh." Morgan laughed and gave Belladonna an affectionate scratch behind the ears. The cat ignored her and continued her writhing, pushing her front paws under the basement door as if there was something playing with her on the other side.

Morgan stood, looking at her watch. "Are you almost ready?"

Celeste sucked down the last of her juice. "Yep. I just need to change and throw on some mascara."

"Well, get a move on." Morgan gestured toward her juice glass. Celeste handed it over, and then pushed away from the island as Morgan rinsed the glass in the sink.

Starting toward the hallway, Celeste looked back at Belladonna who was still batting at the invisible playmate on the other side of the basement door. She'd seen the cat do stranger things after eating catnip, so why did the fact she'd picked this particular door to do it in front of give her such a strange feeling?

Celeste shrugged to herself. She was probably just still spooked from the other day when she'd had to stop the cat from venturing into the basement. She headed off toward the stairs that led to her room, forgetting all about the cat and the basement. She had more important things to worry about today.

4

C eleste caught her reflection in the museum's glass doors. Not bad, she thought. The linen jacket and faded jeans gave her a dressy-casual appearance. Her short haircut always looked trendy, even on days like today when she didn't have time to wash it.

The reflection highlighted the differences between her and her sister. Morgan was taller, her frame more voluptuous than Celeste's thin one which had been sculpted by years of Yoga and Pilates. Morgan's long black hair a stark contrast to Celeste's short blonde crop. The only thing that gave them away as sisters was their ice-blue eyes—the same eyes that all the Blackmoore women had.

Morgan's shoes clicked on the marble floor as they

crossed the vast lobby to the elevators that would bring them to the museum offices. Celeste looked down at her own soft-soled Skechers and wondered if she should have chosen more formal footwear.

The elevator dinged its arrival and the girls got in. Morgan punched the button for the second floor as the doors closed.

"I guess we'll need to see the director. Beasley, I think her name is," Morgan said as the elevator spilled them out onto the second floor.

"Or we could go straight to Skinner's office." Celeste pointed to a placard on the wall that listed the staff members along with the office numbers. Skinner's was 217. The arrow pointed right, so the girls turned in that direction, walking quietly down the hall until they came to a door marked 217. A metal rail was attached to the wall to the right of the door. A faux wood grain nameplate with "Skinner" chiseled in white sat inside the rail.

"I guess this is it," Celeste said.

Morgan wrinkled her brow. "Do you think they just left it unlocked?"

"Only one way to find out." Celeste grasped the knob and turned, her heart skipping when the door opened.

She raised her brows at Morgan who answered

with a shrug and the two of them slipped inside, closing the door quietly behind them.

The office was neat and orderly. Celeste felt a twinge of sadness at the thought of the historian. She pushed aside a pang of guilt for going through his things. It was critical they get his notes on the project and the "key" book back no matter what they had to do to get them.

"You look through that filing cabinet and I'll rifle through the table here." Morgan leaned against a utilitarian steel table that was piled with papers and pointed to an oak filing cabinet next to another, smaller door on the far wall.

Celeste's heart thudded in her chest as she went over and pulled open one of the drawers. The files inside were labeled with letters A-Z. She pushed the files back to reveal the "B" section and her heart jumped when she saw a manila folder labeled "Blackmoore".

"Bingo!" she whispered. Morgan crossed the room as she pushed the folder open inside the filing cabinet, her heart plummeting when it proved to be empty.

"There's nothing in it," Morgan said.

"Did someone take what was in here, or was it always empty?"

"Maybe Skinner hid his notes? If it was *that* important he might not have wanted to just leave them in such an obvious place where anyone could find them."

"If he even *had* notes." Celeste bit her lower lip as she scanned the room for likely hiding places. One wall was covered in a giant green chalkboard—no hiding places there. The wall opposite had an old but sturdy mahogany desk. Built-in bookshelves behind the desk held a variety of books. The wall next to it held the door they came in and the table Morgan had already looked through.

"I guess the desk and bookshelf are the likely places," Celeste said.

"I'll take the desk, you take the bookshelf. Be on the lookout for that poetry book. Without that no one will ever be able to figure out what's in the journal."

The girls went about their various tasks. Celeste scanned through the books, her heart sinking as she realized nothing was the shape, size or color of the poetry book. Behind her she could hear Morgan rummaging through the drawers. The curses her sister muttered under her breath told Celeste that she wasn't having any better luck.

Celeste resorted to taking out each book to rifle through them, just in case Skinner had hidden the notes in a book. She was becoming mesmerized by the task when the squeaking of a door jolted her back to reality.

She whirled around in the direction of the smaller door near the filing cabinet just in time to see it crack open. A dark haired man stepped in. He hadn't seen them yet as he was busy looking back out into the hall. Her heartbeat kicked up the pace.

The man turned to face the room, his dark eyes growing wide when he noticed Morgan and Celeste.

The three of them stood there staring at each other for several rib thumping heartbeats.

"Who are you?" Morgan finally broke the silence.

"Who are *you* and what do you think you are doing," the man replied looking at them suspiciously. Celeste detected a hint of an accent but she couldn't place the origin.

She had to admit, it did seem kind of suspicious what with her thumbing through the dead man's books and Morgan rifling through his desk.

Morgan shut the drawer she had been searching and straightened up. "We're clients of Mr. Skinner looking for our files … and you?"

"I'm Mateo, Mr. Skinners … colleague."

Celeste appraised the man. He was just shy of six feet tall, thick dark wavy hair and dark, velvety eyes that were framed by lashes so long they'd make a super model envious. Even though she got the sense he was lying, his eyes had a sincerity about them that put her off her guard.

They stared at each other for a few more heartbeats.

Finally Mateo said. "Reinhardt mentioned your case to me."

Warning bells went off in Celeste's head. Skinner had seemed like he had the utmost integrity and he'd sworn that he would discuss their project with no one. And how did Mateo know who they were?

"Oh really?" Morgan crossed her arms against her chest. "What did he tell you?"

Mateo answered her question with a question. "Was he able to give you the full details before he died?"

More warning bells went off. *Was he trying to be helpful, or just fishing for information?*

Celeste glanced at Morgan who shook her head slightly. It was too risky to tell him anything.

A loud voice in the hall startled all three of them. It was a voice that made both Celeste and Morgan cringe … and it was coming from just outside the door they'd entered by. Overton.

"I want this office secured. Have you let anyone in here?" Overton's voice boomed into the office.

"No. Not since he … you know …" A woman's voice, much lower.

Celeste's heart jerked in her chest. If Overton found them in there she was sure he'd find a way to use it against them.

Mateo's brows shot up. "I must go."

He turned toward the door he had come in through —the one on the opposite side of the room from where Overton was approaching. Opening it, he quickly glanced out then disappeared into the hall.

Celeste looked at Morgan, raised her eyebrows and nodded at the door. Overton's voice was getting closer. The two girls hurried over to the door and slipped out into the hall following Mateo.

The long, empty hallway stretched out on either side of them. Celeste looked for Mateo, but he was nowhere in sight.

"Where'd that guy go?" Morgan's eyebrows creased together. "I was wondering if we should pump him for information. If he was Skinner's colleague maybe he knows what this important find is all about."

Celeste frowned. "Maybe. But if he *was* a colleague and really did work here, then why did he run out of here as soon as we heard Beasley and Overton in the hall?"

"Good question." Morgan slid her eyes down the hall.

Celeste's heart sank as she looked over her shoulder at the office door. "Well, I guess this was a big fat bust. We didn't get anything."

"We can't go back in there now and Overton's going to have it sealed off, so now what do we do?"

Celeste grabbed Morgan's arm and started down

the hall. "First we need to get out of here before Overton sees us. Then we do the only thing we can do."

"What's that?"

"Come up with plan B."

5

"If the book and notes aren't in his office, then where are they?" Jolene asked, scooping some salsa from the colorful bowl on their backyard patio table onto a chip and popping it into her mouth.

Celeste looked at her younger sister, a frown creasing her face. "I have no idea, but I'm betting he would have stored them someplace safe because he thought this find was important."

"So maybe a safety deposit box, or a safe at his house?" Fiona fished a beer out of the ice-filled cooler sitting beside her chair and popped the top off, flipping it into an empty planter they kept for recyclables. The empty planter sat at the end of a long row of colorful potted flowers blending perfectly into the lush garden atmosphere the girls had worked so hard to create.

Belladonna leapt onto the planter, fished out the cap and started batting it around the patio.

"Possibly. But if so, then how do *we* get them?" Celeste looked across the patio toward the river that was the entrance to Perkins Cove, feeling blessed to have such a scenic view right in their own backyard.

Their property was set up high on a cliff that came to a point where the Atlantic Ocean met the cove entrance. To the left was the open ocean, to the right the wide channel leading to the cove. At the point was a narrow opening that had to be navigated carefully to get into the safety of the cove.

If she craned her neck she could just see part of Perkins Cove about one eighth mile away. The white, wooden drawbridge framed the entrance to the cove which widened out beyond and was dotted with boats —many of them weather beaten New England lobster boats still in use by the fishermen that made their living on the cold Maine waters.

To the right of the cove was a small shopping area lined with cedar shingled fishermen's shacks. Some of them were the original shacks from a hundred years ago, now converted to quaint boutiques and restaurants. She couldn't see the stores from where she sat, but her mouth watered at the smell of fried clams and she could hear the sound of seagulls crying for the tourists to throw them some of their dinner.

"Maybe we can talk to his family … someone must be in charge of his estate now. We could tell them he was working on a project for us and has a valuable book." Morgan swigged her beer. "That sounds reasonable, doesn't it?"

"And if that doesn't work, maybe we can go undercover and pretend we are from the museum … or Jake and I can sharpen our private investigator skills and make a special visit inside his house," Jolene said crunching down on another chip.

Celeste, Morgan and Fiona raised their eyebrows at her. The sisters were glad that Jolene was going to assist Fiona's boyfriend, Jake in his new P.I. business. But they were a bit worried about her attraction for doing things that were a bit outside the law.

As if on cue, Jake came strolling around the house, a six pack of beer in his hand. Celeste's heart warmed at the way Fiona's face lit up when she saw him. Over the summer both Fiona and Morgan had found true love—Fiona with Jake and Morgan with her high school sweetheart, Luke Hunter. Celeste wished nothing like that for herself—her parent's premature deaths had taught her you can't depend on anyone. Still, she was thrilled for her older sisters.

"So, should we hire another historian then? Even though we don't have the poetry book to use as the cipher key?" Fiona asked as Jake scraped a lawn chair across the patio, pushing the back against the table and straddling it with his long legs. He leaned his muscular, tanned forearms on the table, his fist curled around an open beer.

"Well, if you do, you might be signing his death warrant," he said, then casually took a sip of beer.

Celeste's stomach tightened as the four sisters turned their heads toward him.

"Death warrant? What are you talking about?" Fiona scrunched her face at him.

"Your last historian—Reinhardt Skinner—didn't die of a heart attack," Jake said. "He was murdered."

* * *

CELESTE'S BROWS KNIT TOGETHER. "That's impossible. I was sitting right there when he died. He had a heart attack."

Jake put down his beer. "It might have *looked* that way, but my sources in the police department tell me the medical examiner found poison in his blood. The symptoms looked like he had a heart attack, but it was the poison that killed him."

Celeste stared at him trying to process the information.

Could Jake be wrong?

A former police detective from Boston, the girls had

met Jake when he moved to Noquitt to join their small police department. He'd been instrumental in helping Morgan clear her name when she'd been falsely accused of murder. He'd also helped them fend off the treasure hunters who had somehow known there was a treasure to be found on the property and had descended on them this past summer.

Jake was a good guy, which was probably why he and Sheriff Overton had never gotten along. He'd quit the force—actually he'd been forced off by Overton—a few months back. Celeste knew his instincts were good and he wouldn't pass along information like that unless he was sure.

"But why would someone want to kill him?" she asked.

"Could it have been accidental?" Morgan raised an eyebrow at Jake while she picked at the paper label on her beer.

"No. That was what I thought, too, but they said there's no way he could have taken that poison by accident," Jake answered.

"I don't get it. He was such a nice old man. Why would anyone do that to him?"

"Well, isn't it obvious?" Jolene peered at Celeste over her sunglasses. "He told you at lunch that the journal held some information with historical and financial importance. Obviously someone didn't want him telling you exactly what that was."

"But no one else knew he was onto something," Celeste argued.

"Except that guy we saw in his office." Morgan cut her eyes to Celeste.

Celeste chewed her bottom lip. "He did seem to know that Skinner was working for us. But he didn't seem to know the details."

"Come to think of it, how did he even know who we were?" Morgan asked.

Celeste's stomach tightened. "He said that Skinner had told him about our case, but maybe he confused us with someone else. Skinner swore to me that he wouldn't tell anyone what he was working on."

"Wait a minute," Jake cut in. "What guy?"

"We went to Skinner's office today to try to find his notes and the poetry book, and this mysterious guy was there. He acted like he knew what Skinner was working on but also seemed like he was fishing for details," Celeste said.

"He said his name was Mateo and that he was a 'colleague,'" Morgan added.

"Maybe Jolene and I should check him out." Jake shrugged at Jolene. "It would be good practice for our first case."

Jolene's face lit up. "Yeah, I can pay a visit to the

museum and see if I can find out more information on him."

"You guys have a case?" Morgan cut in.

Jake smiled. "Yeah, just a small one for us to cut our teeth on. A cheating spouse. It should be easy … and safe, but a good way for Jo to get some experience. And, of course, the business can use the money."

"Well congratulations," Morgan said, then turned to Jolene. "Just be careful about that Mateo guy. If he's anything like those treasure hunters that came this past summer, he could be very dangerous."

"Do you think it could be those same guys?" Jolene asked.

"I thought they were all killed in the explosion." Fiona nodded in the direction of the hole that had been blown in their yard.

"Maybe there are more where they came from," Jake said.

Celeste's heart sank. The treasure hunters had been ruthless killers … if they, or someone like them, were after something they thought the Blackmoore girls had, it could get ugly.

"Well, the way I see it, we only have one choice," Morgan said, peeling another strip of the label from her beer bottle.

"What's that?" Jolene asked.

"We need to figure out what Skinner was on to and get to it before someone else comes to find it."

"And how do we do that? The key to the cipher is missing and we have no idea where in the journal Skinner made this big find," Fiona said.

"Plus, I don't trust hiring anyone we don't know. I didn't realize the journal would have anything important in it … but in light of what happened to Skinner, it seems like there is. I don't know who we can trust," Celeste added.

"I do," Morgan said grabbing another beer from the cooler. "We have our own history expert who's practically a member of the family."

"Cal Reed!" The other girls chorused.

"Great idea." Celeste wondered why she hadn't thought of calling their childhood friend who was a history buff and antique expert. "I'll talk to him first thing tomorrow."

Morgan put her beer down and leaned into the table. The serious look on her face made Celeste's stomach sink. The words she said next caused a chill to run up her spine.

"We all need to be extra careful from here on in. If these people poisoned Skinner to keep this information secret, there's no telling what they'll do to us."

6

C eleste slid the plastic tray onto the picnic table being careful not to tip over the hotdogs that sat upright in their thin cardboard containers. She sat on the wooden bench seat, feeling the sun warm her back as she scanned the parking lot.

To her left, the *Hot Dog Shack* was in full swing. The roadside stand was aptly named—it really was a small shack, probably older than Celeste but newly painted in crisp white with red trim. The three windows for ordering stood open with lines at each. Tourists that didn't know any better might pass the *Hot Dog Shack* over because it looked like a dive, but the truth was they had the best hot dogs on the East Coast. The lines were always long and the picnic tables that provided the only seating for dining always full.

Celeste had chosen a table far away from the shack, near a stand of trees whose leaves were in the middle of changing from green to orange and yellow. She could smell the earthy, crisp scent of fall and hear the squirrels and chipmunks rustling beneath the trees, gathering their cache of nuts for the long winter.

A smile tugged at the corners of her lips when she saw Cal's vintage 1970 candy apple red Ford Mustang pull into the parking lot. He'd spent the better part of last year restoring the car and it was his pride and joy.

He wore faded jeans and a sweatshirt and managed to capture the attention of most of the female patrons. Celeste laughed to herself as she watched their heads turn to watch him. It wasn't unusual to see this type of reaction. With his tall frame, broad shoulders and boyish good looks, Calvin Reed was a girl magnet. It had been that way since they were teens, although their friendship went back even before that.

Cal's way with women was actually a joke among the Blackmoore girls. And it wasn't only his good looks that attracted them. His family business *Reed Pawn and Antiques* had done very well and Cal was quite wealthy. Combine those with the fact that he was smart, charming and nice and it was no wonder that he was considered the area's most eligible bachelor. He could have his pick of women … and usually did. But

Celeste always wondered why his relationships never lasted very long.

Cal saw her and headed straight to the table, barely noticing the attention from the women. He was used to it by now.

Celeste pushed the tray toward him. "Got your favorite—a chili dog with extra onions."

Cal rewarded her with his crooked smile—the one that made his sapphire blue eyes sparkle and accentuated his dimple. The one that she'd seen him use, quite successfully, to charm many women. As he reached for the hot dog, she noticed his dark tan.

"Did you just get back from somewhere tropical?" she said as she bit into her jalapeño cheese dog.

"Barbados." He wiped a glob of chili from the corner of his mouth.

"Oh, with Janine?" Celeste frowned wondering if she'd gotten the name of his latest girlfriend right.

"Nah, we broke up a while ago. This one was Camilla. Try to keep up, will you?" he teased.

"Well, whoever it was, I hope you had a good time."

Cal shrugged reaching for one of the tall paper cups of soda she'd bought.

"So what's this all about?" He took a long sip through his straw.

She told him about Skinner being poisoned, their

visit to his office and their fears that they might now be in danger from whoever wanted this big find.

As she talked, Celeste noticed the other women were still staring at him, but Cal seemed totally unaware of their attention. His attention was solely on her as if she was the only person that existed. That was one of the things she appreciated most about him— even though he'd never had a romantic interest in any of the Blackmoore girls, he'd always put their friendship first over any prospective dates.

"So there's a real treasure? I thought those caves were empty—the treasure dug up and spent genera-tions ago?" Cal said referring to the warren of passages and caves they'd discovered on their property during the hunt for treasure earlier in the summer. Her sister Morgan had been captured by the treasure hunters and held in one of the caves. She'd escaped by the skin of her teeth just before the whole network of caves and passages had been blown up when the treasure hunters had accidentally tripped the booby trap.

"I guess so. He never got to tell me any details, but he did say it could be historically important and worth a lot of money." Celeste shoved the last of her hot dog into her mouth.

Cal's eyes were bright with interest. "So you want me to help figure out the journal?"

Celeste nodded. If anyone could help them figure it

out, it was Cal. He'd been the one who knew it was a book cipher and he'd helped her decipher some of the passages which led to the whole ill-fated treasure hunt in the first place. She'd known it was a long shot there would be clues to even bigger things in the book. When the treasure hunters had blown up the caves her sisters had thought the treasure was gone and there was not really much use for the book.

They'd hired Skinner out of curiosity to get some insight into their sailing merchant ancestor Isaiah Blackmoore. They figured it would be an account of his travels—she never imagined any of that would be worth killing over.

Celeste swallowed the last of her hot dog and wiped her mouth with a small paper napkin. "There's one problem though ... the poetry book is missing."

"But that's the key. Without it, there's no way to figure out what the journal says," Cal said.

"We're trying to get it back." Celeste shrugged.

"Maybe we can find another one on the internet or something?" Cal offered. "Do you remember the name and edition? I could put some feelers out to the antique book dealers I know."

Celeste felt her spirits rise. "That's a great idea. In the mean time I was thinking we should poke around up in the attic and see if we can dig up anything else that might give us a clue."

Cal sipped his soda, nodding enthusiastically. Cal was an antique expert and Celeste knew how much he loved going in their attic which was loaded with generations of family cast-offs.

Celeste remembered the stern warnings about the attic her mother had given them when they were little. They were all scared to go up there. When they got older, they never paid much attention to it thinking it was just filled with a bunch of old junk. But when Morgan was accused of murder, they needed funds for a lawyer. Fiona had ventured up and come back with a valuable necklace and the discovery of the journal.

They'd eventually made a few more trips up and discovered other items which Cal had helped them appraise. Celeste had always assumed that her mother didn't want them to go up there when they were little because she was afraid they might get hurt with all the junk up there ... but in light of what had been happening, she was beginning to think her mother might have had other reasons to want them to stay out.

"When do you want to get started?" Cal's question pulled her out of her thoughts.

"As soon as we can. If those treasure hunters are the ones that killed Skinner, then it won't take long for them to do something else ... and you know what that means."

"Yeah, big danger," Cal said. "We should start right away—tonight."

Cal pulled his phone out of his pocket. "I just gotta cancel something …"

"A date?" Celeste asked.

Cal nodded as he punched in some numbers.

Celeste's heart crunched—she didn't want him to give up his social commitments for them. "Oh, don't cancel a date for us!"

Cal put his hand over hers and Celeste felt a strange tingle go up her arm.

"No worries," he said. "You're more important than some date … and my heart wasn't really in it anyway."

Celeste listened as he cancelled the date. He was an expert in that too, and was able to do it quickly and sincerely. She also noticed he avoided the other person's attempts to schedule a rain check.

He shoved the phone in his pocket then turned to Celeste.

"Okay, I'm all yours. Let's get started."

7

A shiver of excitement rippled through Jolene as she pulled into the museum parking lot. This was her first time doing "fieldwork" as Jakes P.I. assistant and she was excited to do a good job.

Even though the museum job wasn't for a paying client she still wanted to tackle it as diligently as she would any assignment, even though she knew the real test would come in a few hours when she tried to catch the husband of their first real client cheating with another woman. But, for now, she wanted to focus on trying to find this Mateo person her sisters had talked about.

Glancing in the rearview mirror, she pushed her curly brown hair behind her ears and nodded with satisfaction. That was more professional. Her ice-blue eyes and dark lashes didn't need any help nor did her porcelain skin so she didn't wear any makeup. She hoped that added to the professional look she was trying to project.

She stepped out of Celeste's Volkswagen Beetle, which she'd borrowed for the day. Smoothing her linen pants, she checked to make sure the silk blouse was tucked in. Reaching into the back seat, she picked up a small wallet that held the press credentials her friend at the local paper had made for her. She opened it and peered at the picture of herself rolling her eyes at the name Sandra Storm that was typed below it. Her friend had a strange sense of humor. She shoved it in her pocket, hoping it would be enough to make her seem like she was there on official business.

She headed toward the museum, not the least bit intimidated by the large stone structure. Her platform shoes echoed on the stone steps as she made her way toward the door. She strode through the lobby as if she belonged there, then ducked into the elevator and pressed the button for the second floor.

When she got off the elevator, the placard on the wall told her exactly where to find the director, Anne Beasley. She navigated the hall to her office.

The only word Jolene could think to describe Beasley was "prim". A thin woman of about fifty, she sat ram rod straight behind her desk, her lips pressed together in a tight line.

Jolene knocked on the door and Beasley's lips tightened even more, as if she disapproved of the unexpected visit.

"May I help you?"

"Yes. Hi. I'm Sandra Storm from the Noquitt Tribune." Jolene felt a pang of guilt at how easy the lie flew out of her mouth as she flashed the badge toward the woman. "I'm doing a piece on the museum … well on Professor Skinner and I was wondering if I could get the names of his colleagues—the people he was working with recently."

Beasley stood and came around the desk, her lips pursing even tighter, if that were possible. Jolene hovered in the doorway since she hadn't been invited in.

Beasley reached out for the badge and Jolene's stomach fluttered as she handed it over. She wasn't counting on a close inspection and had no idea if it looked like the official badges.

Beasley studied the badge for several heart thumping seconds, looked up at Jolene, and then back at the badge before finally handing it back.

"I'm afraid I can't give you any names."

Jolene's heart dropped in her chest as the woman turned and started toward her desk

Jolene pulled a spiral bound flip pad out of her pocket. "I have it in my notes that he was working with …" She made a show of flipping through the pad, angling it so the blank pages were hidden from view. "Someone named Mateo. Do you know where I could find him?"

Beasley's thin brows dipped together in the middle. "Mateo? We don't have anyone by that name here. Skinner was working with Penster mostly. You can find her office down the hall."

Beasley jerked her head to the left presumably indicating the direction Penster could be found in and dismissed Jolene by looking back down at her work.

"Okay. Well, thanks." Jolene tried to keep the sarcastic tone out of her voice and started off toward the left.

She walked slowly down the hall. Each office had a metal rail with a name tag slid into it on the side. The door to Penster's office was open and she peeked in.

Penster was the opposite of Beasley. Short, round and dressed in a pink polyester pantsuit. She looked to be ninety if she was a day. Her snow white hair haloed her head in tight curls. She was standing in front of a filing cabinet that was stuffed full. Papers and folders spilled out of the top and sides. Jolene wondered if the drawers actually closed. The rest of the office wasn't much different. Papers were piled on every surface.

Books were stacked waist high around the room. The faint scent of spices and mildew drifted out into the hallway.

Penster turned around, a smile lighting her face when she saw Jolene standing in the doorway.

"Can I help you?" She cocked her head to one side.

"I hope so. I'm from the Noquitt Tribune." Jolene held out the badge and the other woman navigated her way over, dodging the stacks of books and other obstacles that littered the office. She glanced at the badge then back up at Jolene, the smile still on her face but now with her eyebrows raised.

"I'm doing a story on Professor Skinner and I was hoping you could help. I heard you were working with him."

The older woman's face deflated. "Oh, poor Reinhardt. Such a shame. He was a nice man … and a looker too." She winked at Jolene.

"Yes, I'm very sorry for the loss of your colleague."

"I'm Irene Penster," she said holding out a wrinkled hand, the knuckles gnarled with arthritis.

Jolene shook it, surprised at the older woman's firm grip.

"Can you tell me about the project he was working on?" Jolene asked.

Irene pursed her lips and squinted, her wrinkles collapsing into even more wrinkles. "I'm not sure of the details. He mentioned some project about a very old house here in town … something about a sailor. But he was very secretive about it."

"Do you know where he would keep his notes?"

"I believe he kept them in his office. He rarely took work home with him." She turned to a side table which was piled high with papers and produced a box from between the stacks. "Would you like a macaroon?"

"No thanks," Jolene said as Irene slid a tray out of the box and picked out a pink macaroon.

"I was told he was working with someone named Mateo. Do you know where I can find him?"

Irene nibbled the edge of the macaroon, narrowing her eyes as she chewed. "Mateo?" She tilted her head to the side. "No, that doesn't ring a bell."

"Oh well I should be on my way—" Jolene turned to leave, but Irene shoved the rest of the macaroon into her mouth and grabbed Jolene's hand, pulling her into the overcrowded room.

"Would you like to see some of the new Egyptian artifacts I'm cataloging? They are quite fascinating."

Irene pulled her toward the back. Jolene tripped over a round cardboard shipping package and rammed into a stack of books that teetered precariously. She ripped her hand away from Irene, her heart skipping a beat as she grabbed onto the stack to keep them from toppling over.

Irene turned around in time to see the stack of books wobbling, a look of alarm passed across her face, then a smile of relief when Jolene made the save. Jolene stepped backward and held her hand out.

"Sorry, I'd love to see the artifacts, but I really must be going. You know, press deadline and all."

Irene looked disappointed. "Of course. Maybe another time? I do hope your story makes it to press first."

"First?" Jolene's brows mashed together.

"Yes. Didn't I tell you? A man was here yesterday asking the same exact questions you just asked."

* * *

JOLENE LOOKED at her watch as she took the stairs two at a time. She had just enough time to change and get over to the *Knotty Mariner Motel* to catch Mr. Peterson cheating on his wife. Hopefully. Not that she hoped he was cheating, but if he was and she could get a picture then that would mean she and Jake could get their first payment.

Out in the parking lot, she kicked off her platform shoes, then slid into the front seat of the VW bug and twisted around to grab her tote bag from the back seat. She pulled out a pair of old jeans faded to a light blue and so worn they were almost as comfortable as a pair of sweat pants.

Glancing around to make sure no one was watching she wriggled out of the linen dress pants and into the jeans, glad that the doors of the car hid the bottom half of her from view.

While she was contorting herself into the pants, she thought about what Irene had said. Someone else had been asking about Skinner. A man. Could that have been this Mateo guy her sisters met? Irene had said he was a big guy with a bushy beard and an unpleasant demeanor—she'd have to ask her sisters if Mateo fit the description.

She ripped off the silk blouse, thankful she'd worn a cotton camisole underneath and put the lightweight hoodie on over it. She jammed her feet into white flip-flops and settled back in the seat congratulating herself on having the foresight to bring the more comfortable outfit—it was much better suited to sleazy motel surveillance.

She turned the key in the ignition and started to backup, her heart jumping when she looked in the rear-view mirror and spotted a man over in the shadows of the building.

Was he watching her?

She whipped her head around, looking out the back window.

He was!

She wondered if it was the man Irene had told her about but this guy didn't fit the description. He was tall and slim, muscular but not bulky and he didn't have a beard. She noticed his hair was dark and wavy, his dark skin a medium coffee color like he was from a southern climate—Brazil or someplace like that. Her blue eyes met his soft brown ones and she felt a strange tug in her chest just before she ripped her gaze away.

Probably some pervert getting his jollies watching her change in the car. Anger started to boil up inside her. She shoved the car into park, pushed the door open and jumped out facing him ... but he was gone.

"Jerk."

She hopped back into the car, slammed the door shut and headed out in the direction of the motel.

* * *

THE *KNOTTY MARINER Motel* was at the edge of town, down an out of the way back road that most tourists would never find. And even if they did, the broken motel sign and faded paint job would clue them in that it didn't offer the finest accommodations in town. Not surprisingly, the sign announced there were vacancies.

Jolene pulled into the gravel parking lot and backed into a spot at the far end where she could see all the rooms. She got her camera ready as she studied the one story motel which had an office on one end, then ten rooms lined up in a row. Each room had a door with a number and a large picture window, most of them with the drapes tightly shut.

The motel was aptly named. Jolene knew that more than one *naughty mariner* had used it for purposes other than lodging. In high school, kids that grew tired of the backseats of their cars sometimes rented a room for an afternoon and rumor had it that adults seeking company other than their spouse frequented the motel. Which was why she was here, hoping their client's husband would show up with a date on his lunch hour and confirm the wife's suspicions that he was cheating.

She sat and waited. Not much was happening at the motel. The parking lot had a few cars in it, but no one came out of their room. No new cars came in. She found a bag of cool ranch Doritos in her tote and munched them while she watched the squirrels gather acorns and wished that something … anything … would happen. Jake hadn't told her how boring this would be. She had wondered why he was so eager for *her* to do this instead of doing it himself. Now she knew.

She was dozing off when the crunch of car tires on gravel jerked her awake. She crouched down in the seat grabbing her camera. Peeking out of the window, her heartbeat picked up speed when she saw the car was a blue Toyota Corolla—the same car Peterson drove.

The driver's side door opened and a forty-ish, tall, balding man got out. Jolene glanced at the photo on the car seat beside her. Yep, it was him and getting out of the passenger side was a blonde who definitely wasn't *Mrs.* Peterson.

Bingo!

Jolene raised the camera, waiting for the perfect Kodak moment. She watched through the lens as they walked to the office, the man momentarily slipping his arm around her, then letting his hand trail downward until it was on her butt. Jolene tried to get a shot, but they split apart before she could focus. He went into the office while she waited outside.

She ignored the sound of another car pulling in keeping her eye on the woman who was soon joined by Peterson dangling a shiny key from his hand. She kept the camera trained on them as they walked down the row of doors.

Jolene held her breath, waiting for that perfect shot. The couple stopped in front of room number eight. Peterson put the key in the lock then turned to the woman as if he was going to embrace her.

Jolene's finger hovered over the shutter release. The man made his move. She pressed … just in time to get a picture of the two men in the next room walking by with some equipment totally obscuring Peterson and the woman.

Jolene's stomach sank until she realized Peterson was still standing there. She kept the camera poised as she watched him push open the door, then gesture for the woman to enter. As she did, he reached out and grabbed her butt again and this time Jolene got the perfect shot—Peterson playing grab-ass with a woman as he ushered her into a motel room.

A smile tugged at her lips as she put the camera on the seat beside her and turned the ignition on. The picture proved his wife's suspicions were correct. Peterson was playing around. Her first field assignment had been a big success and she couldn't wait to get home and load the pictures from the camera onto her computer so they could get that check from their first client.

8

C eleste paused at the top of the stairs that led to the attic, staring at the dust motes that hung in the slivers of sunlight filtering in through the windows and wondering which way to go. The attic was gigantic. It encompassed the entire fourth floor of their home and was a warren of rooms that used to house servants generations ago. It smelled of dry wood and heat.

There were no servants anymore and each room was stuffed full of various items her ancestors had packed away when they had no more use for them. By the looks of it, the previous generations of Blackmoore's never threw anything away.

She felt a feathery wisp of fur tease her bare calf as Belladonna weaved her way in between her legs and then headed to the left, flicking her tail and looking back over her shoulder at Celeste and Cal.

"Meow."

Celeste shrugged. "Might as well follow her—she usually seems to know just where to go."

They followed the cat past an endless array of bureaus, cribs, tables, hall trees, bed frames, rugs and boxes stuffed full. Cal couldn't help but stop and inspect some of the more interesting items.

"Look at this oak claw foot table."

The excitement in Cal's voice made Celeste turn. She looked in the direction he indicated. A heavy oak table sat there, its surface covered with boxes. The legs, where Cal was pointing, were carved in the shape of giant furry claws, the talons of which grasped onto large crystal balls.

"That's kind of creepy." Celeste wasn't really into old furniture.

"You just haven't developed an appreciation for antiques." Cal squeezed the back of her neck, just like he'd done a thousand times before. Yet something was different this time, although she couldn't say what.

Celeste squirmed away. "Where's the cat?"

"Meow."

Celeste turned in the direction of the sound, feeling a puzzling relief to be not standing so near Cal.

Belladonna had flopped down under a dressing

table in a corner. Boxes and loose items were piled up on either side of it. Celeste looked around feeling a knot of frustration form in her belly.

"I just don't know what we are looking for." Her shoulders bunched with tension as she looked from one box to the next not knowing where to start.

"You seem stressed out." Cal had come up next to her. He turned her around so she was facing away and started working the knots in her shoulders, his strong hands massaging the muscle fibers expertly. She sighed and relaxed against him. He was right, she *was* stressed out … which was not like her at all. But all the pirate treasure stuff from the past summer had been stressful and the thought of it happening again was getting to her.

Before she realized what had happened, Cal had turned her around to face him. Her heart skipped as she noticed how close he was standing. Which wasn't really all that unusual, they'd stood close to each other many times before. So why did she suddenly feel all tingly and warm?

His hands burned on her shoulders. She looked up at Cal, butterflies flapped nervously in her stomach as she saw something in them she'd never seen before. They stared at each other and it was as if time had stopped.

Celeste could feel her heartbeat pulsing in her neck.

Cal's hands tightened on her shoulders.

He moved closer.

Crash!

Celeste jerked away looking in the direction of the sound.

Belladonna sat on the floor behind a silver box which she must have dug out of one of the piles causing it to collapse. Hand mirrors, goblets, gloves and various ladies items littered the floor.

But it was the box that captured their attention.

"This looks like the boxes we found this summer … the ones that held all the clues." Celeste bent to pick up the small silver trinket box.

It was about as wide as her palm and four inches tall. Shiny silver with gold edges and a flower design in high relief. She held it out to Cal.

"It is exactly like the other boxes," Cal said.

Celeste's heart thudded as she studied it. Earlier that summer, the girls had discovered several boxes with the same design. Each box had contained a clue which led them on a hunt for a treasure supposedly buried by the relative who had built the house almost three hundred years earlier—Isaiah Blackmoore.

As far as Celeste knew, Isaiah had been a sailing merchant with a fleet of boats that imported items from the West Indies and Europe. So why would he have buried treasure in their yard? And why the cryptic ledger and treasure hunt with all the clues at various locations?

"Aren't you going to open it?" Cal's voice pulled her out of her thoughts.

She turned the front toward her and carefully pressed the latch. The box popped open to reveal a long silver chain with some sort of crystal pendant on the end.

"What is it?" Cal craned his neck to see inside the box.

"I don't know, some sort of crystal." Celeste picked the necklace up by the chain letting the light blue crystal dangle before her eyes. The sunlight glinted off the facets creating a rainbow of colors inside the attic.

"Maybe Fiona can tell us more about it."

"Tell you more about what?" Fiona said from a couple of feet away, startling both Cal and Celeste.

Celeste turned to see Fiona and Morgan picking their way toward them. She held the necklace and the box up.

"We found a box just like the ones from the treasure hunt and this was inside it."

Fiona reached out and took the stone, her eyes shone as she inspected it. "It's an aquamarine. Rather a large one, too, and absolutely gorgeous."

"Do you think it's from Isaiah Blackmoore?" Celeste asked.

"Maybe a gift for his wife," Morgan said.

"It makes sense that it would be his. Aquamarine is the gemstone of sailors and he was a sailor, right?" Fiona twirled the pendant in front of her, the stone sending sparks of light whirling about the room. "It's worn a lot by travelers to insure a safe passage. Also it can help make the wearer happy and rich."

"Rich?" Morgan looked at the stone. "Maybe we should all take turns wearing it."

"It's also reputed to help with a happy marriage," Fiona said passing the stone toward Celeste.

"Marriage?" Celeste held her hand up, palm facing out as if to ward off the stone. "No thanks."

The girls laughed.

"Hey what are you guys doing home, anyway? Isn't it kind of early?" Celeste wrinkled her brow at the sisters.

Morgan glanced at her watch. "It's four thirty. We closed up a bit early. Luke's coming back tonight and we're going out for an early supper."

Celeste noticed Morgan's big smile and her heart warmed for her sister. Luke Hunter had been Morgan's high school sweetheart but he'd broken things off ten years ago when he'd left Noquitt to serve in the military.

In an odd coincidence, he'd returned to town this past summer on an assignment to fight off the very treasure hunters that had threatened the Blackmoore girls. Near as Celeste could tell, he now worked for a mysterious cartel whose mission was to recover old treasure. His team is sent in to dispense with the pirates who want to take it forcefully and, usually, illegally. The company he works for does all the treasure recovery on the up and up—through legal channels but they still have to fight off the bad guys quite often.

Luke and his team of mysterious men had helped get rid of the pirates that had threatened them, and Luke and Morgan had picked up their romance where they had left off.

"So anyway, about this treasure," Cal said. "I think we should go over all the stuff we found this summer and see if anything new comes up. What Skinner discovered in the journal has *got* to be related."

"We still need to see if we can find the poetry book that will help us decipher the journal." Celeste twisted around to look at the bookshelf where they had found the journal originally. "Where is that journal anyway?"

"I have it safe in my room," Morgan volunteered. "I have a secret hiding spot. No one will find it."

Celeste held up the trinket box. "Let's take this and the necklace downstairs and see if we can put some of the pieces together."

They made their way toward the back stairs, Belladonna appearing out of nowhere to lead the way.

They traipsed single file down the narrow, worn stairway listening to the creaks and groans of the old wood. It dumped them out in the kitchen and they grabbed some tea, coffee and juice before heading to the informal living room.

The house had two living rooms—one was a big formal room with couches no one wanted to sit on and fancy furniture. The other was more comfortable and the room the girls used the most. It was one of the smaller rooms, but cozy with a giant picture window that revealed a gorgeous view of the Atlantic Ocean.

Their mother had decorated the room and Celeste could almost feel her presence in it. The gray and blue decor was soothing and the giant starfish, seashells and rustic painted furnishings with overstuffed cushions made it comfy and homey.

Celeste sank down into the sofa with her glass of green juice, feeling a slight flutter when Cal sat next to her. A little too close. She moved an inch away, annoyed with herself for doing so. It had never bothered her before when he sat close to her. Belladonna hopped up on the couch and settled in Cal's lap, purring loudly as he stroked her fur.

"You guys still have the map, right?" Cal asked.

"Yep, over in the box." Morgan nodded toward a long silver box with the same design as the trinket box Belladonna had dug up in the attic. She didn't need to open the box to know that a leather map sat inside. They'd followed the trail on that map this summer and ended up leading the pirates right to the treasure … or to something that had been rigged to blow a big hole in the cliff.

"But that map led to the cave that blew up," Fiona said over the rim of her coffee mug.

"Right. But maybe we didn't read the map properly. Remember how I told you that sometimes the pirates tried to trick anyone who might come to steal the treasure?"

"Yeah. Except Isaiah wasn't a pirate, he was a shipping merchant," Celeste said.

Cal raised an eyebrow at her. "How are you so sure?"

Celeste's heart crunched. "Well, that's what our mother told us." She looked to her other sisters who nodded.

"Yeah but Isaiah lived three hundred years ago … over the years, the story might have been changed." Cal shrugged. "Because what I see in front of me. The map … the clues … everything seems to indicate that your ancestor wasn't a sailor … he was a pirate."

9

"**W**ho was a pirate?" Jolene appeared in the doorway with a paper cup of coffee from Starbucks in her hand.

"Cal thinks our great-great-great-great-great-grand-father was a pirate," Morgan said.

"Cool!" Jolene plunked down in one of the over-stuffed chairs and turned to Cal. "Why do you say that?"

Celeste explained Cal's reasoning, still not sure if she was on board with it. From what she knew, pirates were nasty thieving killers and she wasn't sure she wanted to be related to one.

"That makes total sense." Jolene nodded. "So what are you guys doing?"

"We found this in the attic." Celeste pointed to the

trinket box and necklace that were lying on the coffee table in front of her. "So we're going over all the clues we found this summer."

"Those clues led to the map in the box which we thought was pretty straight forward," Cal cut in. "But what if the map wasn't really a map of your yard like we thought it was?"

Celeste pressed her lips together. "Well, then what would it be of?"

Cal shrugged. "I guess that's what we need to find out. But it makes sense. If Isaiah was a pirate then he might have done the map in some sort of code."

"Maybe the map isn't even the *real* map," Morgan offered. "The poem in the lining of the box could be a clue to where the real treasure is."

Morgan crossed the room and opened the box. She took out a small fragile piece of paper, placing it on the coffee table. Celeste looked down at it, reading the faded words written in old style script.

THE SEA IS MY LOVE,
The Ocean's Revenge lies below my love.

"WE KNOW his boat was called the *Ocean's Revenge* from the manifest we found," Fiona said referring to the copy of an old ship's manifest that had been found in the pocket of one of the treasure hunters who'd shown up dead on their cliff. The manifest had listed the vessel's name with Isaiah Blackmoore as captain and a listing of the cargo the ship carried.

"So, this note seems to imply the *Ocean's Revenge* lies below the sea," Jolene said.

"But I thought the treasure hunters already scanned the ocean out there and came up empty." Fiona thrust her chin in the direction of the Atlantic.

"Is it possible they just didn't look in the right place?" Jake appeared in the doorway, then crossed to Fiona's chair then pulled her long red curls away from the side of her neck and planted a kiss on it. Fiona's cheeks turned pink and she looked quizzically at him.

"You left the front door open, so I let myself in," he explained.

"It's possible they missed it," Morgan said. "But I thought they scanned the ocean floor out there with sonar or something. If they didn't come up with anything it seems likely nothing is out there."

"Yeah, could be." Cal pressed his lips together and Celeste noticed how that made his dimple even deeper and more appealing. "It could also be hidden down there—camouflaged somehow. Back in the day, pirates often sunk their own ships in shallow water so that no one else would get the booty. Then they'd simply dive for the treasure when they wanted some."

Celeste narrowed her eyes toward the ocean. "Is it *that* shallow out there?"

Cal shrugged. "I think it's definitely a lead we should follow up ... unless you guys have a better idea?"

"We should also follow up on getting another poetry book. We *need* to figure out what Skinner was on to," Morgan said.

Celeste turned to Jolene. "Speaking of which, how did you make out at the museum?"

Jolene made a face. "Not so good. The director said there is no one named Mateo there."

Celeste's stomach clenched. "What? So who was the guy we saw, then?"

Jolene shrugged. "No idea. But I talked to someone Skinner worked with ... Irene somebody or other and *she* said that a man had been there the day before asking questions about Skinner."

Celeste's heart did a somersault. "What did he look like?"

"Big guy with a bushy beard and a bad attitude. Is that your guy?"

"No. Ours didn't have a beard," Celeste said. "Maybe you guys can sharpen your private detective skills and try to find out who he is?"

"Sure we'll get right on that," Jake said glancing at Jolene who nodded in agreement.

"Speaking of which," Jolene said. "I think I got the evidence we need for our first client."

"That's great," Celeste said, her heart swelling with pride for Jolene, who was obviously bursting with excitement.

"Yep, caught him almost right in the act and I have the pictures on my computer. Wanna see?"

"Of course," Jake said. The sisters nodded.

Jolene sprang up from the chair and sprinted out of the room.

"Okay," Celeste said. "We should make a list of things we need to do in order to figure out what Skinner's big find was, before those nasty treasure hunting pirates come for it."

As she turned to get a pen and paper from the table under the window, Luke appeared in the doorway. The grim look on his face froze her in her tracks.

"It's too late for that," he said. "They're already here."

* * *

"HERE?" Celeste's heart thudded against her chest as she glanced outside looking for bad guys moving in the tree line.

"At the house?" Morgan sprang out of her seat.

"No, no." Luke held his hands up in front of him, palms out. "I meant in town. But they're looking for treasure that's connected with your land, so they'll be here eventually."

"How do you know that?" Jake asked.

Luke pushed Morgan back down in her chair and leaned his well-formed butt on the arm. "I just came from a meeting with the head honchos and I got a new assignment. Imagine my surprise when I found out it's here in Noquitt—and not just anywhere in Noquitt … right here at your house."

Celeste narrowed her eyes at him. "How do they know those treasure hunting pirates are here?"

Luke took a deep breath. "I don't really know how they get their information. There's some kind of underground treasure network. I just know what they tell me. By the way, you guys really should lock your front door. I was able to walk right in."

Celeste's heart skipped … Luke and Jake had both just walked right in which means the treasure hunters could too. She peeked out into the hallway half expecting to see a band of pirates rushing toward them.

"I'll lock it," Fiona said, then disappeared out into the hall.

"Word about Skinners find must have gotten out.

That's why they're here," Cal said.

"And *they* are probably the ones who poisoned him." Celeste returned to her seat on the couch with pen and paper in hand.

"Well, at least one thing is good," Jake said.

"What's that?" Fiona came back into the room, her eyes narrowed at Jake.

"Luke's already assigned to stop them so we'll have extra help," Jake said.

"Yeah, we'll protect you guys from them, but you still need to be on high alert. I don't have to remind you of how dangerous these people can be," Luke warned.

Jolene skittered into the room, laptop in hand and stopped short.

"You guys look like you just ate bad seafood. What's wrong?" She turned, noticing Luke on the arm of Morgan's chair. "Oh, hi Luke. Let me guess … you bring bad news."

"Afraid so." Luke shrugged, holding his arms out at his sides. "Seems the pirates are back and they think you still have something worth taking here."

"Well, that's not really a big surprise, is it? I mean considering what happened with Skinner and all," she said sliding the laptop onto the table by the window.

"True," Celeste said. "So now we need to really get our act together and come up with a plan."

"Well, like we said before, Jolene and I will try to find out who this Mateo person is." Jake turned to Luke and explained how Morgan and Celeste had gone to Skinner's office and run into the mysterious Mateo.

"He could be one of the pirates and if the pirates are here because of what Skinner found, then we need to know what that was," Luke said.

"So we need to either find his notes, if he had them, or decipher the book ourselves," Morgan added.

"I don't think we're going to find his notes." Celeste tapped the end of the pen on her front tooth. "So we need to find that poetry book—the cipher key."

"Did anyone write down the name of the book and what edition it was?" Cal asked.

Everyone shook their heads.

"I didn't write it down, but I think I remember." Jolene closed her eyes. "It was green, with gold lettering ... leather ... dated 1717. The title was *Grayson's Poems* and it was the fourth printing."

Celeste, scribbled the name down on the paper then stared up at her sister. "You remember all that?"

"Yep, I just close my eyes and picture it."

"You must have a photographic memory," Cal said. "That would really come in handy in the antique business."

"Hey, watch it pal. I've already hired her for the P.I business," Jake joked.

Cal laughed. "I can contact some of the rare book dealers and see if they have that edition."

"I think we need to put together a plan to check out the ocean." Morgan pointed to the poem on the table. "That seems to imply something is … or was … out there."

"I can do some scuba diving out there and check things out in person. Maybe I'll find something that sonar didn't detect," Celeste offered, excited about being able to put her scuba experience to good use.

"That sounds like a good start." Cal glanced at the list Celeste had in her lap. "Find Mateo, Find the poetry book and check the ocean."

"Yeah, that's plenty for now. In the meantime, my team will try to ferret out where these pirates are staying," Luke said.

"Sounds like a plan. Now let's talk about something positive. Jolene closed our first case today—a cheating spouse." Jake nodded at Jolene. "Let's see the evidence."

Jolene turned the laptop screen to face them and clicked a few keys. The monitor was filled with a picture and she clicked the mouse to scroll.

"Oh, sorry. Not that one—some guys got in the way." She scrolled to the next picture which showed Peterson and the blonde in the open motel room door. "That's it!"

"Perfect." Jake reached out to shake her hand.

"Wait a minute," Luke said. "Go back to that other picture."

Jolene scrolled back. Luke leaned forward in the chair.

Celeste narrowed her eyes at the picture. In the background she could see Peterson in front of the hotel room. In front of him two men carried some equipment.

"That looks like an underwater metal detector. Where did you take this picture?" Luke furrowed his brow at Jolene.

"The Knotty Mariner … out on Belton Road."

"Those could be our bad guys." Luke's lips were pressed in a line as he pulled out his cell phone. "I'll have my men go check it out."

"Wow, that would be cool," Jolene said. "Maybe you'll be able to catch them and we won't have to worry about them coming here."

Luke looked at her grimly as he punched numbers on his phone. "We may be able to catch *them*, but I'm afraid that won't solve our problem."

"Why not?" Celeste's brows mashed together, her stomach sinking as she anticipated his response.

"Because, from what I heard, this is just the recon crew. There's plenty more coming."

10

C eleste jerked awake, pulling her feet back from the cold, wet pressure that rubbed against them. She blinked the sleep out of her eyes, her heart skipping when she saw her grandmother sitting on the end of her bed. Well, not her flesh and blood grandmother—she'd died years ago—this was the ghost of her grandmother, a white vapor that looked just like the real thing ... except for the fact she was mostly transparent.

This wasn't the first time grandma's ghost had visited her, but Celeste still felt a little disturbed when she saw the wispy figure. Belladonna, on the other hand, seemed quite at home with grandma's ghost and lay on her back, her paws batting at the charms that dangled from the apparitions charm bracelet.

"Well, good morning sunshine!" Grandma said in her usually cheery voice. Apparently death agreed with her.

"Morning Nana." Celeste scuttled herself back in the bed, pulling the sheets up to her neck.

Grandma went over to the window and the drapes parted themselves to let the morning sun in. She stretched her arms wide, smiling at the view. "It's a beautiful day today!"

Celeste squinted at the window, shading her eyes against the beams of sun that brightened the room.

"Yeah. Sunny," she managed to say, still a bit put off by the sudden appearance of her grandmother jolting her out of her sleep. Her stomach lurched when she looked at the clock beside her bed. It was eight thirty. She had two yoga classes to teach this morning before she went to the dive shop to rent scuba tanks.

"I better get up." She slid her legs out from under the sheet, touching her feet flat on the hard, wood floor.

Grandma turned from the window, her arms crossed against her chest. "I won't keep you dear. I just came to tell you to be careful."

Celeste's stomach crunched. Her grandma might be a ghost, but it was nice to know she still cared.

"Thanks ... so you know about all this pirate stuff?"

"Of course. Being dead does have its advantages."

Grandma waved a hand in the air, the charms on her bracelet tinkling. "But, I'm afraid evil forces are at work against you. You and your sisters will need to use all your skills to fight them."

"Skills?" Celeste's forehead pleated between her brows.

Grandma nodded. "Yes, you girls are stronger than you know."

Celeste glanced at her biceps—they *were* rather muscular for a girl. Being health conscious, she worked out a lot and had great muscle tone from teaching Yoga at the studio she co-owned.

Grandma looked at her curiously, then crossed to the bed and sat down beside her. Goosebumps stood up on Celeste's arm in reaction to the chilly vapor of Grandma's ghost. "Things aren't always as they seem, Celeste. You should try not to take them so literally."

"Okay," Celeste said, wondering exactly what that meant.

Grandma cocked an ear toward the wall, apparently hearing something only ghosts could hear. "Well, I must be going—it's time for the party.

"Party?"

"Yes. We have a lot of them in the afterlife. It's quite a bit of fun … once you get used to not having a physical body. Anyway, I wanted to come and warn you to be on your guard."

"Okay, thanks Grandma." Celeste felt the urge to give her a hug but wasn't sure how that would work out. Her arms would probably just pass right through the vapor. Plus she wasn't sure of the proper etiquette when dealing with ghosts, so she simply stayed seated on the bed.

"Celeste, keep in mind … what you seek might be right underfoot." Grandma stamped her foot on the floor. Then she disappeared into a cloud of fading mist, leaving a chill in the room and a slightly damp spot on the bedclothes as the only evidence of her visit.

* * *

JOLENE PARKED her Dodge Dart across from Reinhardt Skinner's house, swearing under her breath when the car stalled out before she could turn it off. She had a love-hate relationship with the car. She loved that it was paid for, but hated that it barely ran. But what did she expect? The car was older than she was.

She wasn't supposed to be at Skinner's but her internet search for the mysterious Mateo had come up blank. Since he'd already been to the museum, she figured he might show up here. She'd talked to Skinner's brother who had said they wouldn't start to clean out the house for another two days, but he'd promised to take a look tomorrow and see if he could find the

Blackmoore notes or poetry book. Which meant no one should be at the house today, and she'd had a feeling it might be smart to come and take a look.

She wasn't going to get out, or anything, just sit here and watch. Too bad she didn't know what Mateo looked like … only that he didn't have a beard.

The house was small, a one story ranch with an attached garage. Looking at the house from her vantage point in the car, she could just barely see the side. It didn't take long for her to notice something seemed a little off. Was the door to the garage open a crack?

She craned her neck to be sure, her heartbeat picking up speed. She knew she shouldn't go over, but couldn't think of a reason why the door would be open. The driveway was empty, so it wouldn't be any of Skinner's relatives. Maybe one of them had left it open by mistake. She should at least shut the door, shouldn't she?

She crept over to the side of the house. Her instincts told her this might not be a good idea. But it was the middle of the day. What could possibly happen in broad daylight?

Splintered wood around the latch told her the door wasn't left open by mistake. Someone had broken in. She found herself wishing she'd finished that gun safety course, gotten her permit and had a nine millimeter in her purse. The safest thing would be to run back to the car and call Jake or the police.

But she didn't. Instead she pushed the door fully open and ventured into the garage.

"Hello?"

Her voice echoed in the small space which smelled of gasoline and concrete. It was cool in here, and a shiver ran up her spine. No one answered.

The door to the house was open just an inch. She picked her way toward it.

When she was halfway there, the door pushed open toward her. Jolene's heart leapt into her throat as two men came through. They didn't notice her at first— they were focused on a notebook the first man carried. The second man pointed to something in the book, his huge biceps flexing as he did. The first man bent his head to look closer at the notebook, his long beard almost touching it.

Jolene froze on the spot, her brain sent messages to her legs to run, but her legs didn't seem to be receiving them.

The two men looked up from the book, stopping in their tracks when they saw Jolene standing in the middle of the garage.

They stared at each other for three long heartbeats before the men sprang into action throwing down the notebook and rushing toward her.

Jolene's heart sank as her legs tried to scramble backwards, to escape the grasp of the thigh sized arm that was hurtling toward her. Suddenly she regretted not taking those karate classes that Celeste always tried to push on her.

"No!" She yelled out the word instinctively holding her hand out in front of her with the palm up facing her attacker. Her mouth opened in surprise when the man was propelled backwards, as if by some unseen force, then slammed against the garage wall.

"Holy crap," the other guy said echoing Jolene's thoughts.

Jolene didn't have long to think about how the guy could have possibly been thrown against the wall like that because he had recovered and now both guys were rushing toward her. She turned to run, but her feet slipped on something slick. She felt someone grab her as her legs went out from under her. Then her head exploded in pain as everything went dark.

The next thing she knew, she was lying on the damp earth outside the garage and had the distinct impression someone had been grabbing her butt.

"Are you all right?"

She looked up into velvety brown eyes that were laced with concern. The world swam into focus and a hint of recognition sparked in her brain.

Her heart jerked in her chest and she pushed away from the stranger who had been kneeling beside her.

"You're the pervert from the museum!" She scrambled to her feet backing away from him.

"What? I'm not a pervert," he soothed. "I came to help you."

"Help me my ass … I felt you touching my butt!" Jolene dug in her pocket for her cell phone. "I'm calling the police."

The stranger's eyes went wide. "No, don't."

"Yeah, right," Jolene said as she dialed.

The stranger glanced to the side, then back at Jolene. Their eyes met and she felt mesmerized, her fingers frozen on the keypad of her phone.

"We will meet again," he said. Then he slipped around the corner of the house.

She ran after him, not quite sure if his words were a threat or a promise.

"Hey, don't think you can get away with—" But when she rounded the corner he was gone.

She stood alone in the yard, in total silence. Looking around, she wondered what happened to the big guys from the garage. She glanced at the door—it was shut, the wood damage still evident but the door securely in place. She tried to open it, but it was locked.

Peering inside, she could see the door leading to the house was closed and there was no evidence of the skirmish in the garage ... nor of the notebook she'd seen them carrying.

Could those men have been the treasure hunting pirates?

Her palm tingled as she remembered how the man had been thrown against the wall. Feeling an icy chill creep up her spine, she crossed the street to her car, her thoughts turning to the brown eyed man.

Had he been following her? She was sure it was the same guy she'd seen at the museum. But who was he and why would he be *here*? Did he have something to do with all this treasure stuff?

Was he in cahoots with the men in the garage? And if he was, what happened to them? And what was in the notebook she'd seen them with?

She gave one final glance at Skinner's house as she got into her car. She stuck the key in the ignition and pumped the gas pedal, praying the old car would start. She couldn't get out of there fast enough.

11

Celeste's bare feet scraped against the rough wood of the dock as she contorted her arm behind her shoulder to zip up her wetsuit. The sea air stung her nostrils and the familiar sound of the ocean rushing over the pebble beach and clutching at the stones to try to drag them back into its depths was like music to her ears. She loved the sea and scuba diving was one of her favorite pastimes.

A small motorboat she'd borrowed from a friend bobbed in the water at the end of the dock while Morgan and Buzz, one of Luke's men, loaded diving gear inside. Luke had insisted they take the brick wall of a bodyguard with them even though Celeste had argued the girls were more than capable of handling themselves.

"Ready?" Morgan asked as Celeste climbed into the boat.

"Yep." Celeste took the seat in the back while Morgan moved to the driver's seat. Buzz grunted and sat in the bow scanning the open ocean with a pair of binoculars. Celeste was learning that he was a man of few words.

"So where do you want to dive?" Morgan steered the boat out of the small cove that housed their dock and into the open ocean facing the cliff next to their house. From the ocean, the hole from the blast looked raw and jagged. The grass at the top spilling over the edge, the newly exposed rock was lighter in color—a sharp contrast to the rock on either side that had been exposed to the weather for centuries.

Celeste squinted at the cliff which rose almost a hundred feet above them. She didn't see any evidence of the caves or passages. Had they all caved in or been sealed off during the blast?

"I guess we should start right here." She indicated the section halfway between where they'd come from and the point of land that marked the entrance to Perkins Cove. "This is the deepest part. I don't know if one could get a ship up near the point."

Morgan cut the motor and dropped anchor. Celeste checked the oxygen tanks one more time, then bent to pick one up.

"Need some help?" She looked up, surprised to find Buzz at her side.

"Sure," she said. He lifted the tank and helped her strap it on, then went back to his watch in the bow.

Celeste sat on the edge of the boat to put on her flippers while mentally prepared herself for the cold water. The Maine ocean could be shockingly cold even in summer, but now in fall it would be frigid. Her wetsuit would help, of course, but it would still be cold. She double checked her gloves and booties to make sure she had as little skin exposed as possible.

Morgan knelt down in front of her and grabbed her wrist. "Be careful down there … I have a bad feeling like you might get lost or something."

Celeste made a face.

Morgan put her hand up. "I know you're a very experienced diver but my gut feeling says you should be careful. Don't go too deep or anywhere that is too dark."

Celeste remembered how Morgan's gut feelings had saved them from being attacked earlier in the summer. They'd been walking down the street when she'd had one of those feelings and pulled Celeste back from an alley opening. If she hadn't, Celeste might have walked right into an ambush. Morgan's gut feeling had helped them escape unharmed. Her grandmother had told her to encourage Morgan to trust her gut feelings more, clearly grandma knew something they didn't. What Morgan had was more than just intuition and Celeste took her words seriously.

"I'll be careful. Thanks." She smiled at her sister then nodded in a signal that she was ready to dive.

Stuffing the mouthpiece into her mouth, she tumbled backwards into the cold, silent underwater world of the Atlantic Ocean.

She floated for a few seconds acclimating her body to the chill and getting her bearings. The open ocean was to her left, the cliff to her right. It was rocky here and she had to be careful not to let the motion of the waves slam her against the rocks. She dove down deeper where the movement was calmer.

The water was clear. She looked from side to side, not really sure what she was looking for. A sunken ship? A treasure chest? She saw a lobster in a sandy patch on the bottom and wondered briefly if she should snag it for supper, deciding against it when she realized she'd feel bad for days knowing she'd had the power of life and death over the poor creature and chosen its death.

She swam along the edge of the rocks toward the point hearing only the steady sound of her own breathing as she took the stale oxygen into her lungs. Gliding over an outcropping of rocks, she kept her eye mostly on the bottom, looking for anything that didn't seem natural in the crystal clear water.

A sense of calm pulsed through her as she swam about twenty feet below the surface. She loved the peaceful feeling of being underwater. The quiet. The graceful movement of the fish, seaweed and other sea creatures.

Something wrapped around her ankle. She jerked her foot away, but whatever it was held on.

Probably a long strip of seaweed, she thought as she turned to untangle it from her foot. She felt a tug on her heart as she saw a shadowy figure, its arm outstretched toward her ankle. She kicked out with her free foot, pulling the other one back as forcefully as she could but that only caused the grip to tighten.

Panic seized her chest. Bubbles cascaded out of her mouth as the figure seemed to materialize before her eyes. A bearded man. One of the treasure hunting pirates? Celeste's mind whirled as she kicked harder, furiously trying to get away.

The man was shaking his head, waving his arm. With a jolt, Celeste realized he didn't have any scuba gear on.

How could he possibly be under water without gear?

She stopped struggling long enough to notice that he seemed like he was trying to tell her something. She watched as his body shimmered in the water, almost transparent. He seemed to be pointing to the ocean floor below.

She looked down, her eye catching the sparkle of something round. The pressure around her ankle eased and she dived down reaching out for the gold object. A coin. She turned it over in her hand recognizing the cross design as being the same as the old Spanish coin they had dug up in their yard earlier in the summer. What had Cal said it was? An Escudo or something like that. Very old and very valuable. She put it in her dive pouch.

The bearded man swam in front of her. Beckoning for her to follow. She was reluctant, but curiosity took over. She swam after him, noting his odd outfit—a white billowing shirt, tan pants that were torn on the bottoms. The impossibility of him being underwater without a scuba outfit or oxygen tank hit her like a face full of ice water.

He was a ghost.

He didn't seem to be a threat so she followed. His movements were more like gliding than swimming. He never kicked or moved his arms as he pushed forward, his long hair floating behind him. Celeste felt a seed of doubt in her stomach when she realized he was moving toward the point where the entrance to the cove was. Surely this water was too shallow for a shipwreck?

He stopped about fifty feet short of the point, looking back to make sure she was still there. He smiled and then turned west, heading straight into the cliff. Celeste cringed as she imagined him crashing into the jagged rocks of the cliff. Do ghosts feel pain? Maybe he would just pass right through the rock like those cartoons of *Casper the Friendly Ghost* she used to watch when she was a kid.

But he didn't crash or pass through. He was standing on something, motioning for her to come closer. Her chest tightened when she realized he was standing in the mouth of a big cave.

She swam forward just enough to get a good look. She never knew there were caves in the cliffside and this one was a whopper. She couldn't see very far in though—it was too dark.

The ghost tilted his head toward the back of the cave in a motion that Celeste took to mean he wanted her to follow. She remembered the warning Morgan had given her before the dive and she floated in place, every muscle telling her to go back to the boat.

The ghost glided out to her, reaching out for her wrist but she pulled away. Her eyes wide inside the mask, shaking her head "no." A look passed over his face—sadness? He floated back into the cave, and his body disappeared slowly as if it was evaporating into the water and Celeste was alone.

Her heart kicked when she checked the gauge on her air tanks. She had just enough air to get back to the boat. She turned back in that direction wondering just what was in the cave and why the ghost seemed so intent on leading her in there.

12

"How was the scuba dive?" Jolene paused with a forkful of carrot cake midway to her mouth, as she looked at Morgan and Celeste in the kitchen doorway.

"Unusual," Morgan said sliding into the chair next to Jolene at the kitchen island.

Jolene's mouth was busy chewing cake, so she simply cocked an eyebrow at Morgan in response.

"I saw a ghost underwater," Celeste said as she hunted in the fridge.

"Underwater? I didn't know they could go underwater." Jolene scraped a thick blob of cream cheese frosting from the top of the cake and licked it off the fork. Earlier in the summer, she'd been a bit taken aback when Celeste had mentioned she had seen their grandmother's ghost, but after several reported sightings it didn't really faze her much anymore. Especially after what happened in Skinner's garage earlier that day.

"Apparently they can." Celeste pulled her head out of the fridge, a bag of spinach and a plastic container of mixed fruit in her hand. "And he led me to a huge underwater cave out by the point."

"What was in it?" Jolene asked.

"I don't know. I didn't go in." Celeste dumped the ingredients into the high powered blender along with ice cubes and water and turned it on.

"Oh and I found this," Celeste yelled over the motor as she dug the coin out of her pocket and put it on the island in front of Jolene.

Jolene picked up the coin noticing how smooth it felt as she turned it over in her hand.

"This looks like a Spanish treasure coin—like the one we dug up in the yard this summer," she said after Celeste turned off the blender and she was able to hear again.

Celeste nodded as she sipped her drink.

"So there *is* a treasure down there." Jolene glanced out the window toward the ocean. "We'll have to watch out for those guys from the *Knotty Mariner* and their underwater metal detectors."

"Yeah, Luke has some guys on watch over there to make sure no one comes in by boat," Morgan said.

"What about you? Did you have any luck with the search for Mateo?" Celeste asked Jolene.

Jolene blanched. "Not really, but I think I ran into the pirates."

"Ran into them? Where?" Morgan's eyes were clouded with concern.

"Well … I happened to drive by Skinner's house and I noticed the side door to the garage was open," Jolene started.

"Why did you go there?" Celeste cut in.

"Just checking the house, you know to make sure no one broke in." Jolene looked down, pushing the crumbs on her plate around with her fork. "Anyway, there were two gigantic guys with beards taking a notebook out. I thought it might be from Skinner's journal. I tried to stop them and something very strange happened."

"You tried to stop them?" Morgan's eyes were wide. "That seems dangerous."

Jolene shrugged. "Yeah, I probably should have run away but I put my hand up to ward them off and I felt this rush of energy through my palm. Then one guy flew backwards and crashed against the wall. It was weird," Jolene said wiping her tingling palm on her jeans.

Celeste narrowed her eyes at Jolene. "You mean like some sort of paranormal force?"

"Yes. Exactly. Why not? You see ghosts, Morgan has intuition and we all saw what Fiona's healing crystals did for my arm." Jolene looked down at her arm which had been cut badly when the treasure hunters had broken into their home earlier in the summer. Fiona had wrapped it for her and put one of her crystals—a carnelian—in the wrapping. The next day, the cut had been totally healed. "So, I don't think it's so weird that I have some special ability too, is it?"

"Not at all." Celeste pressed her lips together. "I wonder if that's what Nana meant."

"Huh?"

"I was talking to her—well her ghost—this morning and she said we were stronger than we know. I wonder if she was talking about our strange abilities. Maybe there is more to them than we realize," Celeste said.

"Well, I don't know how useful it is," Jolene said. "I have no idea how to make it happen again."

"Is that how you got away from the pirates, then?" Morgan asked.

"No. At least I don't think so. After the guy got slammed into the wall, they were coming after me and I tried to run, but I slipped and blacked out. The next thing I knew, I was outside and some pervert was feeling me up."

"What?" Morgan and Celeste gave her identical looks, their brows rising to meet their hairlines.

"Yeah, some weird guy was there and I felt him touching my butt." Jolene put her hand on her backside, right where she remembered the man touching her and heard the crunch of paper. Her forehead creased as she reached into her back pocket and pulled out a wrinkled piece of note paper. She didn't remember putting anything in there.

"What's that?" Morgan asked.

"I'm not sure." Jolene spread it out on the top of the island.

"It looks like some sort of maze." Celeste bent over the paper which showed a series of passages laid out like a maze along with lines and arrows. It was recently hand drawn in pen on white lined paper. "And a map of how to navigate it."

Morgan reached out, picking up the paper and holding it in her hands. She closed her eyes for a second. When she opened them, Jolene felt her heart skip at the serious look they conveyed. "We're going to need this. I don't know why but I have a feeling that it's important."

"Do you think it has something to do with the treasure?" Jolene asked.

Morgan nodded.

"We better keep it safe. Maybe you can put it with the Journal, Morgan," Celeste said.

"Okay. I'll take it up right after we're done here." Morgan put the map back down on the counter so they could study it some more.

"Meow." Belladonna stole their attention from the paper.

"Hi, Belladonna." Morgan slid out of her seat to pet the cat who sat in front of the basement door staring at them and flicking her tail.

"I have no idea why but she seems to be obsessed with that basement," Celeste said.

"Maybe it's because of this." Fiona came into the room holding a dustpan out in front of her like it was filled with toxic waste. Jolene craned her neck to see what was in it and understood why her sister was holding it that way when she saw the two headless mice.

"Ewwww." Celeste, Jolene and Morgan scrunched their faces.

"Where did you get those?" Celeste asked.

"They were on the front porch. Neatly lined up in front of the door. Like a gruesome present."

The four of them looked at Belladonna who puffed up her chest proudly.

"You think she's getting mice from the basement?" Morgan asked.

"Maybe." Fiona shoved the mice into a trash bag securing it tightly and heading in the direction of the outside trash barrels. "We should have one of the guys check it out and see if she is getting in from some window or opening and secure it. We don't want the treasure hunting pirates to have an easy way in."

"I'll talk to Luke," Morgan said as Fiona shoved the bag outside.

"What's that?" Fiona joined them at the island, pointing to the map of the maze.

"We're not sure ... a map of a maze or something." Jolene told her what had happened at Skinner's.

"So you think that guy put it in your pocket?"

Jolene pressed her lips together. "Maybe that was why I woke to find his hands on my butt."

"Who is he?" Fiona asked.

"No idea." Jolene shrugged.

"What did he look like?"

"He had a dark complexion. Like maybe he was from Brazil, or Cuba or something. Dark wavy hair and dark eyes. And a slight accent."

Jolene saw Morgan and Celeste exchange a glance. "That sounds like the mysterious Mateo."

"Well if it is, I think he's following me because I also saw him staring at me in the museum parking lot," Jolene said.

Fiona's forehead creased. "Why would he follow you?"

"Who knows. Apparently he must be connected to this whole treasure thing somehow," Jolene said.

"Sure seems that way," Fiona agreed.

"Yeah it sure does," Celeste added. "But the question is, whose side is he on?"

* * *

"I DIDN'T FIND any openings where someone could get into the basement." Luke shoved a pair of thick gloves halfway into his back pocket and bent down to brush dirt from his knees. He motioned for Celeste and Morgan to get up from where they sat, on the front steps of their porch, and follow him around the side of the house.

He pointed to the granite slabs that sat under the cedar shingle siding. "Your foundation is really old. There's no windows or even a bulkhead. There's really no way for a person to get in, but there might be some cracks a cat could wriggle through. Anyway, I don't think we need to worry about pirates getting in that way."

"Speaking of pirates," Celeste said. "Did you have any luck at the motel where Jolene took the pictures?"

Luke rubbed his hand over his chin, the day old

stubble making a rasping noise as he passed over it. "As a matter of fact, we did. You won't have to worry about *those* two, but more will be coming. From what little information we could get, it seems there is some big deal about a really low tide. I guess they have some plan that centers around that."

A shiver crawled up Celeste's spine. "Low tide? I read that Friday there's going to be an unusually low tide—the lowest one in almost three hundred years. Dead tide, they called it. Something about the alignment of the sun and the moon."

"We figure they'll be coming from the open ocean. I guess there really is some treasure sunken out there." Luke thrust his chin toward the Atlantic.

"So we only have three days?" Morgan squinted at Luke.

"Seems that way. I have my men positioned to watch the Atlantic so if anyone comes in that way, we'll know about it."

"What about that underwater cave I saw the other day?" Celeste asked.

"We'll check that out too. I have some guys that know how to dive and we're going to scour the area tomorrow," Luke said. "Do you want to dive with us?"

Celeste made a face. "I'd like to, but I have Yoga classes most of the day. What's with this whole low tide thing, though?"

"Maybe the treasure is too deep at high tide?" Morgan offered.

"Maybe, but if so that would mean it was further out—not near the cliff," Celeste said.

"I'll make sure my guys check the deeper waters— even if we can't get to it until Friday, we should be able to *see* if something is there," Luke offered. "But in the meantime, we really need to start trying to figure out what Skinner knew so I can get an idea of what those pirates have planned. It could help us ward off the attack."

"Do you think that map of the maze is a clue?" Morgan raised her brows at Luke. They'd shown him the paper that had been placed in Jolene's pocket earlier and he'd been as mystified as they were.

Luke shrugged. "Possibly. But where is this maze?"

"Could it be underwater? Maybe Isaiah hid the treasure in the rocks or something and that map shows how to get to it," Celeste said.

Morgan wrinkled her brow. "The maze seemed a little too geometric to be from the natural rock, but maybe Isaiah rearranged the rocks or carved out crevices."

"That would make sense. I'll look for any abnormalities in rock structure while we are out there." Luke draped his arm over Morgan's shoulders and nuzzled her neck.

Celeste took the hint and turned back toward the front of the house, cautiously looking for dead mice as she walked up the steps. She pulled the door open, taking one last glance out over the ocean, all the while her stomach sinking, an imaginary stopwatch ticking off the seconds in her mind until the treasure hunting pirates descended on them.

13

The next day, Celeste found it difficult to concentrate on yoga. She finished her classes early and headed home right after. Slipping in through the front door, she shrugged out of her light jacket and slipped off her shoes. The yoga classes she'd taught earlier in the day had left her feeling an odd combination of drained and refreshed. She needed some wheat grass juice and an apple before she relaxed into her afternoon meditation.

Padding into the kitchen in bare feet, her heart stopped when she looked toward the basement door. It was wide open. *Was someone down there?*

Celeste crossed cautiously to the door. Neither her nor her sisters ever went into the basement, the door was never open like this, in fact they usually kept it locked. Maybe Luke had opened it yesterday when he was inspecting it? She was sure the door had been closed tight last night and Luke hadn't been back since.

She peered down the stairs into the darkness.

"Hello?"

"Mew." The sound was so faint she wasn't even sure she'd heard it.

"Belladonna?" Was the cat down there hurt?

"Mew." Another pathetically soft meow filtered up from below.

"Are you hurt, kitty?"

Celeste felt a tug at her heart. The cat could be down there stuck or injured. She could have fallen in the well or gotten into something. She *had* to go down —no matter how scared she was.

She groped along the wall lightly looking for the light switch, her shoulders tensing, her arm getting ready to pull back if her fingers encountered anything crawly or slimy. She found the hard plastic switch and flicked it, peering down into the basement which was now slightly dim instead of pitch black.

She stepped lightly on the first step, then the second. The cold air of the basement came up to surround her as she slowly descended the steps. The damp musty smell tickled her nose. Her eyes strained to get used to the dim lighting.

"Belladonna?" She stood with her left foot on the bottom step, her right hovering in the air, uncertain whether she should continue or turn and flee back up the stairs.

"Meeew." The sound came from her left. Celeste's heart crunched—Belladonna sounded weak as a kitten.

Looking in that direction, she could barely see something white in the corner. The cavernous basement was lit by one low-wattage bulb which hung from the ceiling about twenty feet away, the arc of light barely reached the area from where the sound came.

Her stomach fluttered as she stepped off the last step. The compacted dirt floor of the basement felt damp and clammy on her bare feet. She realized she should have put shoes on before venturing down. Too late now, she thought as she tip toed her way across the floor toward the cat.

"Mew." Belladonna greeted her as she approached. The cat was wedged behind something big and round. It was almost as tall as Celeste and about three feet wide. It sat against the wall.

"Belladonna, are you okay?" She bent down to pet the cat and was rewarded with a loud purr. "Did you get stuck?"

She stood up to inspect the offending piece. It was hard to see the details in the dark but she could make out that it was wooden and round like a barrel with metal bands. A big giant wine cask. She tried to move it, but it wouldn't budge. It looked ancient and she wondered if there was still wine in it. Why else would it be so heavy?

She peered around to where it was wedged against the wall, her heart jerking when she came face to face with a swirly white mist. A ghost. And not just any ghost, the very same one that had lured her to the cave entrance during her dive.

She jumped back and the ghost looked insulted. His long dark, wavy hair hung down to his shoulders. Who was he?

"Hi," she ventured, still keeping a safe distance.

He waved then reached out his hand, causing her to jump back a little further. Then he inclined his head toward the wall, beckoning to her with his index finger just like he had when he was trying to get her to swim further into the cave.

Celeste frowned at him. Did he think she could go through the wall like he could?

He reached out and grabbed her wrist. Her heartbeat picked up speed as she felt a cold mist wrap itself around her hand, the chill working its way up her arm. Her pulse drummed in her ears as she tried to pull away while he tried to pull her toward the dark crevice where the cask met the wall.

She heard a faint knocking. Was that coming from the cask?

The ghost nodded at her. The knocking got louder. She peered around the edge of the cask, feeling along the wall. It was wet and not all that pleasant. She jerked her hand away. Her heart beat faster.

The ghost glanced up, then said, "Ooops," and disappeared into the dark crack between the cask and the wall leaving only a slight swirly mist in his wake.

"What the heck?" Celeste looked up but didn't see anything, then realized the knocking was turning into a pounding and it wasn't coming from the cask. It was coming from upstairs … the front door.

She glanced over at Belladonna who slipped out of the crevice and ran upstairs.

"Stupid cat wasn't even stuck," she muttered as she headed toward the front door to stop the incessant pounding before it gave her a migraine.

Belladonna was already at the door, arching her back and hissing. Celeste shoved her aside and ripped the door open, her heart plummeting when she saw Overton standing on the other side, his fat knuckles raised toward the door in mid-knock.

"What do *you* want?" She glared at the sheriff.

He rocked back on his heels, a satisfied smirk spreading across his face as he reached into his back pocket and pulled out a piece of paper.

"I wouldn't be so uppity if I were you." He waved the paper in her face. "You and that dark haired sister of yours are suspects in a murder case and this here is a warrant to search the premises."

Celeste's heart skipped. "Murder? What murder?"

"Reinhardt Skinner." Overton tried to push his way past her into the house, his foul breath assaulting her nose, the toothpick wiggling up and down between his lips as he stared at her with rheumy eyes.

Celeste barred his way by wedging her body in the door, her hip on one side and her arm stretched across to the other. "What? We didn't kill Skinner—a dozen people saw me sitting with him when he died. And I tried to revive him!"

"*Conveniently* sitting with him when he was *poisoned*, you mean?" Overton raised a bushy brow at her.

"What? That's ridiculous. You can't get a search warrant on that flimsy evidence. You have no *legitimate* reason to suspect me or Morgan!"

Overton's laugh chilled Celeste's blood. "Actually, I have two. Skinner was poisoned with aconite … that's a poison that comes from a plant. Wolfsbane. That plant is growing right out in your garden."

He paused, jerking his head in the direction of Morgan's herb garden. Celeste pressed her lips together. Was that the toxic plant Morgan had warned her against?

"And if that wasn't enough," Overton continued on, "We found your fingerprints, *and* those of your sister, all over Skinner's office."

14

O verton tried to push Celeste out of the way, but she held her ground. They were grappling in the doorway like a pair of angry lovers when Delphine Jones' Toyota Camry skidded to a stop in the driveway.

Overton stopped battling Celeste and they both turned to see Delphine leap out of her car and run up the walkway. Her loose purple jacket flying out behind her reminding Celeste of a super-hero come to save the day. How did she know to come here at the exact right time?

"You hold it right there Overton!" Delphine narrowed her eyes at the sheriff and received an unfriendly scowl in return.

Delphine was the area's best lawyer and had helped the Blackmoore girls on several occasions, most of which involved Overton wrongly accusing them of something and trying to put them in jail. Delphine and Overton were arch-enemies, the feisty attorney never missed an opportunity to make him miserable.

"I have a warrant." Overton held up the papers.

"Let me see that." Delphine grabbed at them and Overton handed them over reluctantly.

Jake's Suburban came racing into the driveway, stopping beside Delphine's car. Morgan, Fiona and Jake tumbled out, charging up the steps to join them.

"Are you okay?" Morgan asked Celeste.

Celeste nodded. "What are you guys doing here?"

"I heard about the warrant being issued," Jake said earning a venomous glare from Overton. "Fiona called Delphine and we got here as fast as we could."

"There's a problem with these." Delphine looked up at Overton. "I'm afraid you'll have to come back later with the proper papers."

Overton frowned at the petite attorney. "What do you mean? Everything should be in order. I had judge Sanderson sign it and everything."

"Yes, but he didn't sign in the right place." Delphine pointed to a spot on the paper.

"What? That's just a technicality," Overton sputtered, his face turning red.

Delphine shrugged, handing the papers to him. "Well, we have to follow the letter of the law. I'm afraid you'll have to get Sanderson to sign it properly before I can let you invade my clients' home."

Overton's face twisted with anger as he grabbed the papers from Delphine. "Have it your way. But I *will* be back this afternoon and I *will* find the evidence I need."

He fixed Celeste with an angry glare as he stormed down the steps and into his squad car where two of his uniformed officers had been waiting.

They watched him drive off then Delphine turned to Celeste. "What's this about?"

Celeste puffed out her cheeks. "As usual, Overton wants to pin a murder on us. This time it's Reinhardt Skinner, a historian we hired to look at one of the old journals we found in the attic."

"He was murdered? What evidence does he have to tie it to you?"

"He was poisoned," Celeste said. "According to Overton, the killer used aconite."

Morgan's breath hitched. "Aconite? But that's from the wolfsbane plant."

"Yeah, and Overton said we have that in our garden."

"We do," Morgan said. "It has certain medicinal properties, but if abused can be toxic."

"So he got a search warrant based on the fact you have this plant growing in your garden? Is it uncommon?" Delphine swiveled her head between Celeste and Morgan.

"Not really," Morgan said. "I mean not everyone would have it but I'm sure this isn't the only place in Maine where the plant is growing."

"That wasn't the only thing," Celeste said. "He also found our fingerprints in Skinner's office."

Celeste saw realization spread across Morgan's face. "From when we were there looking for the book?"

Celeste nodded.

"But that seems flimsy too," Morgan said. "We hired him so it makes perfect sense we would have been in his office."

Celeste was glad she left off the part about how their trip to his office had been *after* he died.

"You're right. Both of those are flimsy." Delphine waved her arms like a purple bird. "But somehow Overton got a judge to sign off on a search warrant. I don't doubt that he's up to no good though—I've suspected that since he came to this town."

"Me too," Jake said.

"Well at least, you got rid of him for now." Celeste looked at her watch. "But I wonder how long it will take for him to come back. He only needs to go across town to see the judge. He could be back in an hour."

"Oh, he won't be back today." A sly smile spread across Delphine's face. "I happen to know that

Sanderson is playing golf all afternoon. He won't be back in chambers until tomorrow morning."

Celeste's shoulders relaxed slightly. "That's great. So we have the rest of the day. Although I don't know what we need it for. We aren't guilty of anything. But somehow I feel like Overton is going to find something to make us *look* guilty and we have to figure out what it is and make sure we don't have it."

"Don't worry. I'll be back here first thing to make sure he doesn't overstep his bounds and to counter any of his bogus findings," Delphine assured them.

"Well, thanks so much for coming. You're a life saver." Celeste hugged the other woman and they went through a round of good-byes before Delphine got into her Toyota and sped off.

Fiona turned to the others, her arms spread at her sides. "Now what do we do?"

Celeste puffed out her cheeks. "I guess the only thing we can do is go over what we know about Skinner and this whole treasure business so we're prepared to deal with anything Overton may come up with."

"We need this like a hole in the head, what with the pirates coming in three days." Morgan glanced nervously toward the ocean.

"I wish I knew why Overton was so hell bent on pestering you guys," Jake said.

"Me too." Celeste's stomach churned and she remembered how hungry she was. "Let's call Luke and Cal and see if we can get their input. I could use a snack while we are waiting for them. Anyone want some wheat grass juice?"

15

No one else wanted wheat grass juice, so Celeste made some for herself and then filled a bucket with water to soak her feet which were black with the dirt from the cellar floor. She was relaxing on the front porch swing with her feet in the bucket when Cal's mustang pulled into the driveway.

He looked comfortable in worn jeans and a half zipped faded blue hoodie over a navy blue tee shirt. The night was cool, but not cold. The ocean breeze ruffled his hair slightly as he walked up the porch steps. When he sat down on the swing beside her, Celeste felt a wave of relief spread over her. Cal always made things seem better when they were going wrong … and things were going very wrong right now.

"What's with the feet?" He gestured toward the bucket.

"Oh, I had to go rescue Belladonna in the basement and I was barefoot. It's a dirt floor down there and my feet were filthy. I'm trying to get them clean, but I think they might be turning into prunes by now." She lifted one foot halfway out frowning at the puckered white skin.

Cal leaned over, grabbed her foot and wrapped it in the towel she'd had beside her on the swing just for that purpose. He rubbed it dry, then put it in his lap and massaged it gently, causing a flurry of strange tingly sensations to flood Celeste's belly. Which was odd because she'd never felt this way before. Well, at least not with *Cal*. He was a friend, nothing more. Besides, he had way too many women on his plate as it was and she didn't want to be just another notch. Her odd feelings were likely just a reaction to all this crazy stuff going on around them anyway.

She pulled her foot away, her heart crunching at the hurt look on his face.

"So what did you guys want to talk about?" he asked.

She took her other foot out of the bucket and grabbed the towel, rubbing the foot dry as she told him about Luke's discovery that the pirates were going to come at low tide in three days.

"Yeah, I remember reading something about that. It will be the lowest it's ever been, but why is that significant?"

Celeste shrugged. "I have no idea. All we can figure is that the treasure might be somewhere that you can only get to at the low tide."

"Would the low tide expose some sort of beach or sandbar? You know, one that would be impossible to dig out when it was underwater?"

Celeste straightened in the seat. "You know, that's not a bad idea. I'm not sure where one would be though—I've never seen an exposed beach or sandbar. The water all around here is over fifty feet deep. Do you think the tide could get lower than that?

"Don't know. I've never really looked at the shore during low tide here. When I swim, I go to Noquitt beach, but you know how far the low tide goes out there—stands to reason the same would happen here."

Celeste shook her head. "When we were little girls, we played near the water all the time and we never saw a sandbar. But maybe the tide was never anywhere near this low."

"Right." Cal studied her. "Did something else happen? You look really stressed."

Celeste told Cal about Overton's visit, her stomach sinking lower and lower as she relayed everything that happened. When she finished, she was practically in tears.

"I'm sure he'll be coming here first thing tomorrow and we'll have to deal with that while trying to figure out where the treasure is before the pirates get here."

Cal put his arm around her, pulling her in close. His arm felt warm and comforting and a little more than just friendly.

"Don't worry. Between all of us, I'm sure we'll figure something out." His sapphire eyes studied hers, his free hand coming up to trace the line of her bottom lip causing her stomach to flip over.

"But what if he arrests us?" she whispered.

"I'll make sure he doesn't," Cal said. Then he leaned in and the next thing she knew his lips were brushing hers.

Celeste felt like time had stopped. Her lips seemed to have a mind of their own as they reacted to Cal's kiss by pressing closer against his. They surprised her by parting slightly and her tongue, which apparently had its own ideas, darted out to meet his.

She sighed and relaxed into the kiss, listening to the evening sound of crickets, smelling the clean scent of ocean breeze and tasting the spicy taste of Cal's lips.

And then her brain kicked into gear. *What was she doing?* Cal was like a brother to her—although there was nothing brotherly about his kiss, or the way his hands were starting to explore her body. She had to admit, it wasn't all that unpleasant. She realized it had been way too long since she'd dated anyone.

But, the *last* thing she needed right now was to get involved with someone—especially someone who had a "little black book" the size of the bible. She needed Cal as a friend more than anything. Plus she wasn't interested in a short fling with anyone, and certainly not with someone as important to her as he was.

Her brain managed to get a signal through to her hand, which she discovered had somehow entangled itself in Cal's hair, and she put her palm flat on his chest. She felt the warmth through his shirt … and hard muscle. She briefly wondered what the rest of him felt like but then common sense took over and she pushed harder with her palm.

Cal broke the kiss, looking at her with confusion. "What's wrong?"

Celeste raised her brows. "Wrong? You kissed me."

Cal smiled, leaning in for more. "Yes, and I plan to do it again."

Celeste scrambled away from him. "I don't think this is such a good idea."

"Why not?"

"We're *friends*. I don't want to screw that up."

Cal bit his lip, his eyes clouding over with something. Disappointment? He reached over and took her hand. "We could be more than friends …"

Celeste pulled her hand away and shot up out of the chair.

"I don't think so. I'm not one of your disposable girlfriends. I would hope you would think more of me," she said, then turned and ran into the house.

"Celeste wait," he called after her. "I do think more of you."

She didn't hear him. Her mind was whirling with emotions and questions. Part of her wanted to run as far away as her legs would take her but with everything going on here, she couldn't let her sisters down. She slowed her pace and stilled her mind, then headed for the informal living room. Her ears vaguely registered the sound of the front door opening behind her as she entered the room.

* * *

LUKE, Jake and her three sisters were gathered in the informal living room. They lounged in the overstuffed chairs and on the sofa. Fiona had a piece of paper and a pencil and they looked like they had been busy formulating a plan at one time. Except now everyone was staring at her … or did it just feel that way?

"Is everything okay?" Morgan asked.

The heat crept up Celeste's neck into her cheeks. "Yes. Fine. What's going on?"

"I thought I heard someone yelling," Luke said.

"Oh, hi Luke. When did you get here?" Celeste asked trying to turn the focus of the conversation away from *her*.

"I've only been here a few minutes. Came in the kitchen door."

Cal came into the room just then and Celeste skirted behind the chairs standing, arms crossed, next to the window on the other side of the room.

Celeste noticed her sisters ping-ponging their eyes between her and Cal and her cheeks got hotter.

"So, are you guys working on a plan?" She asked hoping to steer the conversation to something important.

"Well, the way I see it, we have two problems. Overton's search tomorrow and the bigger problem of these treasure hunting pirates," Jake said.

"Whatever the pirates are after can only be accessed at this really low tide that is happening in three days," Luke said. "But that doesn't mean they won't actually come here sooner. My men have been able to get some more information from the guys we caught at the hotel and it's worse than we thought."

Celeste's stomach sank. She didn't want to know *how* they were getting information from the motel guys or what they planned to do with them after, but this didn't sound good. "How so?"

"They work for a particularly nasty fellow named Goldlinger." Luke took a deep breath. "We've tangled with him before and he's not afraid to have his minions kill to get what he wants. I'm afraid they might come early and try to get you girls out of the way."

"By *out of the way*, you mean kill us, right?" Jolene asked.

"Afraid so."

"Wait a minute," Jake said. "What did you say the guy's name was?"

"Goldlinger."

Jake pursed his lips. "When I worked for Overton, I used to eavesdrop outside his office. I knew he was up to something and I figured the more ammunition I had about him the better. I heard him addressing someone on the other end of the phone as Goldlinger—not once but several times."

Celeste's heart kicked. "You don't think Overton is in on it with this Goldlinger guy?"

Jake shrugged. "It sure would explain a lot."

"Yes, it would," Morgan said. "Like why he's always trying to put us in jail."

"To get us out of the way," Fiona added.

"And that might be why he's so keen on getting this search warrant," Cal said. "If he is in on it with

Goldlinger, he might be trying to search the house for the journal or other clues."

"Right." Jolene leaned forward in her chair, elbows on knees. "We know they have the notebook they took from Skinner's and possibly the cypher key—the poetry book—but they probably don't have all the pieces to piece together the location of this big find of Skinner's"

"Ironically, they're in the same boat as us," Jake said. "We have the pieces they need and they have the pieces we need."

"And Overton could be after those pieces," Celeste said. "He's probably not even looking for anything to do with Skinner's death—he's coming to search the house for clues to the treasure."

Cal looked at Celeste from across the room. "Well, if he is coming to look for clues, then I say we give him exactly what he wants."

* * *

CELESTE SCREWED UP HER FACE. "Are you crazy? Why would we do that?"

Cal laughed. "Not the real clues, fake ones. Something that will throw them off track."

Luke nodded. "What a great idea. That's brilliant."

"Yeah, but *what* fake clue? We don't even know

what the real clues are, how will we know how to fake one?" Jolene asked.

"Let's figure out what we *do* know," Morgan said.

"We know there's some big find—we'll call it a treasure since Skinner said it could be valuable," Celeste answered.

"And we know that there's already bad guys here looking for it, for some reason the low tide is significant, and apparently they don't know all the information they need to figure out where it is." Jolene ticked the three items off with her fingers.

"And we have the journal and a mysterious map of a maze," Celeste added then turned to Luke. "Did you guys find any sign of treasure or an underwater maze on your dive?"

"No, we didn't see even anything that could come close. We did find an old brass cross and some pewter mugs scattered around the ocean floor, but no treasure."

"What about that cave?"

Luke raised his brows. "That was interesting. The opening is gigantic, but the top is about twenty feet down so you would never see it from the ocean. Anyway, we swam in quite a ways—it goes into the cliff pretty far but part of it was blocked with rubble."

"From the explosion earlier in the summer?" Jolene asked.

"Maybe. I'm not sure. We had to back out since we'd been diving all day and the oxygen was running low."

"Did you see any sand bars out in the ocean?" Celeste asked remembering her conversation with Cal and then feeling her cheeks grow warm again.

Luke shook his head. "No. Why do you ask?"

"I was just wondering if this whole timing with the lowest tide might be because a sandbar is exposed— you know somewhere that would be easier to dig up a treasure if it wasn't covered in water."

Luke rubbed his chin with his thumb and forefinger. "You know that's not a bad theory. We should get a geographical map of the ocean floor all around the cliff." He pulled out his cell phone and punched in a text.

"So we still don't know where this maze is … or even how it is connected," Celeste said.

"Can I see this maze map?" Cal asked.

"Sure." Morgan stood up. "I put it with the journal in my secret hiding place upstairs. I'll run up and get it."

"So, where do you guys think this maze is anyway?" Fiona asked.

Everyone shrugged.

"It must be here, on or near our land or the pirates wouldn't be coming here," Celeste said.

"Do you think Skinner discovered exactly where it is?" Morgan asked as she slipped back into the room, placing the maze map on the coffee table in front of where Cal was seated.

"Hard to tell." Luke stood behind Cal and looked down at the map. "If he did, the pirates probably know exactly where it is too."

"But if they do, why wouldn't they just be here now digging it up?" Jolene's brows mashed together as she stared at Luke.

Luke gave a half head shake-half shrug. "Either they can't get it because of the level of the tide ... or they are waiting for the final piece of the puzzle."

"What's the final piece of the puzzle?" Fiona asked.

"The map that shows exactly how to get *to* the treasure," Cal said tapping his index finger on the maze map.

"You think that's what the map shows?" Jolene squatted down on the other side of the table.

"Sure. See these arrows and thin lines?" Cal traced his finger along the lines on the map. "These show you what path to take in the maze."

"So the thicker lines are the walls of the maze?" Jolene asked.

"Yes, it looks that way." Cal narrowed his eyes across the table at Jolene. "Did the man that gave you this say anything about it?"

She shook her head. "No. I didn't even know he had slipped it into my pocket until later."

"Well, it has to have some significance to this whole treasure thing. This could be the very map that leads us to the treasure," Cal said.

"Or it could be a ruse—something to throw us off track," Celeste argued.

"No. I have a feeling it's very important. This isn't a ruse." Morgan looked at Celeste and then at the others. "I have a very strong feeling about it."

"Okay then. If Overton is working for Goldlinger, this could be exactly what he is looking for," Jake said.

"So we make a fake map and hide it somewhere that Overton will find it. If we're right, then the pirates will end up following the wrong path in the maze and come up to a dead end and no treasure." Jake thumped Cal on the back. "Excellent idea."

"So, based on what we know, it would seem the pirates know where the maze is but not how to navigate it and we know how to navigate it but not where it is," Celeste said.

"Right," Luke said. "If Overton bites on the fake clue, then we'll know for sure that he's in on it with them."

"The fake map will keep them from getting to the treasure, but it won't solve our immediate problem," Jake said.

"You mean that the pirates could come to *get us out of the way* any time now?" Jolene asked.

Jake nodded, causing Celeste's heart to sink.

"That's why we need to find that poetry book right away," Cal said. "Because our only hope now is to find the treasure first *before* they have a chance to hurt the girls. And in order to do that, we need to decipher the journal just like Skinner did."

16

Celeste stared out the front window, her stomach churning in anticipation of Overton's arrival. Her gaze wandered over to the porch swing that she and Cal had sat on the night before and her heart pinched. He'd left last night without even saying good-bye to her. Was pushing him away what she really wanted? She wondered if she'd done the wrong thing and lost her best friend.

From her vantage point at the window she could see the road that led through Perkins Cove to their driveway. Her shoulders tensed as the Noquitt police cruiser rounded the corner to the cove and sped its way down the road toward her. It pulled to a stop in front of her house and Overton lumbered out with two uniformed officers behind him.

"I'll handle him." Delphine, who had arrived moments before, opened the front door greeting Overton with a stony face and an outstretched hand. Overton pushed the papers toward her, hitching up his pants and chewing on his toothpick as Delphine inspected them, her mouth set in a grim line.

She glanced over at Celeste and her sisters, who had now gathered in the entrance way, then handed the papers back to Overton.

"They're in order. We'll have to let him in." She stepped aside and held the door open.

Overton passed through the door pausing only to aim a menacing glare at Celeste and her sisters.

Overton pointed to one of the cops. "Blake, you take this floor, I'll take the second floor and Towers can take the third floor."

The two cops nodded and took off to their respective floors. Celeste exchanged a look with her sisters. Overton hadn't mentioned the attic which she thought was weird, but she was grateful since she didn't want him messing around with their family heirlooms.

Overton disappeared down the hallway toward the stairs leading to the second floor.

"Meeeyowl!"

"Damn cat!" Overton's voice bellowed through the house.

Celeste suppressed a giggle when Belladonna came

skittering into view, unharmed. She must have inadvertently gotten in Overton's way on the stairs. Belladonna winked at her lazily and she wondered if the cat had known exactly what she was doing.

"I got some fresh blueberries, who wants to make blueberry muffins?" Morgan raised her brows and gestured toward the kitchen.

Celeste's stomach nagged, reminding her she had forgotten to eat supper. "I do."

"Me too," Fiona and Jolene said at the same time, and then punched each other lightly in the arm.

"I'm going to make sure Overton and his gang don't do anything inappropriate," Delphine said, turning in a flurry of tangerine and yellow. The feisty lawyer was known for her colorful outfits and today she'd chosen a loose tangerine jacket made from some semi-sheer material which topped off a yellow shirt and yellow, orange and pink skirt. Quite a contrast to her black yoga pants and white tee-shirt, Celeste thought as she followed her sisters into the kitchen.

"Celeste, you grab the ingredients. Jolene, get the muffin cups and pan. Fiona, grab the mixer and a big bowl." Morgan directed from the stove where she was preheating the oven.

Celeste assembled sugar, flour, baking powder, milk and butter on the kitchen island. Fiona put the large stainless steel mixing bowl from their KitchenAid mixer beside them. Morgan brought over a measuring cup and measured out the ingredients, dumping them in the bowl in turn.

"We'll fold the blueberries in by hand after this is all mixed together." Morgan pointed to a pint of over-sized blueberries that sat on the kitchen counter as she fitted the steel bowl in the mixer base, lowered the paddle and turned it on.

The sisters had a row of blueberry bushes that grew on the cove side of the yard. It was well past blueberry season now, but they always picked the bushes clean in the season and froze them for later. Morgan must have taken these out of the freezer last night.

Celeste leaned over in her chair, grabbed one and popped it in her mouth. An explosion of juicy sweet tartness coated her tongue as she bit down.

"These are really juicy," she said, then stuck out her tongue. "Ids my ton boo?" The words came out garbled, but her sisters knew what she meant.

"Yes," they answered in unison.

Celeste crossed her eyes trying to look at her tongue to see how blue it was.

A crash came from upstairs and they all flinched as they heard Delphine yell at Overton.

"You better not break any of my clients' things or you'll be paying for it."

"It was that damn cat knocked it over." Overton's voice echoed down to them. "It's not broken."

The girls tore their eyes from the ceiling and Morgan started folding the blueberries into the batter while Jolene plunked a thin pleated paper muffin cup into each section of the pan. Fiona poured the batter into the muffin cups and they shoved the pan into the oven.

Then they took a seat at the kitchen island and waited.

Mixing the muffins had been a nice diversion but now they could hear the sounds of the search going on and Celeste's heart grew heavy with dread.

Jolene broke the silence. "I wonder what he's going to take."

"He'll probably take the opportunity to steal some of our good stuff," Fiona said.

"I wouldn't be surprised." Morgan scowled at the ceiling.

"Well, at least there's nothing that he can use to incriminate us," Celeste added.

"I'm just glad I brought my laptop over to Jake's," Jolene whispered. "If he took that I'd be out of business."

Celeste nodded. They'd brought more than Jolene's laptop over to Jake's. The leather map and the silver box was over there as well, along with the poem they'd found in the lining and the real map of the maze. The fake map which they'd made last night was "hidden" in the fireplace in Celeste's room. They'd carefully drawn it in the same color pen on the same paper, taking care to make the path exactly the opposite of what it was in the original map. Luke had installed an inconspicuous camera directed at the spot, so they'd be able to tell right away if Overton took the bait. He was monitoring it from his apartment downtown.

Morgan's cell phone erupted in a cacophony of chirps and tweets. She glanced over to where it sat on the kitchen island to see the message.

"It's Luke." She didn't need to elaborate. The other girls knew what it meant. Overton had taken the map.

* * *

"Towers, are you 'bout done up there?" Overton bellowed from the second floor. Seated in the kitchen, the sisters could hear the front stairs groan under his weight as he descended them.

"Come on Blake, hurry it up." Overton's voice carried into the kitchen from the library. The timer on the oven dinged and Morgan took the muffins out just as Overton appeared in the door with Delphine and Blake behind him.

"So you're done then?" Delphine queried Overton.

"Yep." The toothpick bobbed around in his mouth as he eyed the steaming muffins.

"I'll need a copy of the inventory sheets," Delphine said. Celeste had seen them carry out a few bags during the course of their search. Everything the police took would be catalogued and written down. Celeste would bet good money the map of the maze wouldn't be on the list.

The sound of footsteps running down the stairs and into the hall announced Tower's arrival. Overton turned and looked at the two cops.

"Did you get everything loaded into the car?"

Towers and Blake nodded.

"Then I think we're done here." Overton's gaze shifted to the kitchen window and his eyebrows went up. "Except for one last thing."

He took an evidence bag out of his pocket and started toward the back door motioning impatiently for Towers and Blake to follow. Without a word to Delphine or the sisters, he ripped open the door and stomped out into the garden.

Celeste watched as he trampled basil, chives and chamomile on his way to the far corner. He paused and pulled a sheet of paper out of his pocket—it looked like a printout with a picture. Squinting at the paper he leaned down to get a better look at the plants. After a few minutes, he found his target—wolfsbane. He ripped the wolfsbane plants out of the ground and shoved them the plastic evidence bag.

Morgan flinched at the callous treatment of her herbs.

"Gee, I hope he didn't get any on his hands. He might accidentally poison himself," she said sarcastically as they watched him walk toward their driveway, the two uniformed cops following him like obedient baby ducks.

Delphine snorted out a laugh. "Okay, well if you guys don't need me I have to get back to the office."

"I don't think we need you and thanks for coming. Want a muffin?" Fiona held a napkin wrapped muffin out.

"Sure." Delphine took the muffin. "I'll get you a copy of the inventory list as soon as Overton gets it to me. And I'll keep my ears peeled for any more warrants."

"You don't think he's going to arrest one of us, do you?" Jolene asked. "You know, like he usually does."

Delphine rolled her eyes. "Unless he comes up with something concrete, I don't think he can. It's weird though … he didn't take very much out of the house today."

Celeste peeled the paper off the sides of her muffin. *That's because he was really only after one thing.*

"If he does try to arrest one of you, I'll have you out

in a jiff." Delphine held the muffin up with a nod, then turned and disappeared toward the front door.

"Looks like Overton really *is* working for this Goldlinger guy." Jolene's eyes shone with excitement.

"I guess he has been all along," Morgan said.

"Yeah, all this time he's been trying to get us out of the way. Trying to frame us for murder and doing things so we would have a hard time paying the property taxes." Fiona twisted the crystal bracelet on her wrist as she talked.

Celeste remembered how hard it had been to come up with the tax money on the seaside mansion before they'd discovered that they had some very valuable pieces in the attic. Overton had taken every chance he got to turn the screws on them so that they would struggle for money.

"I wonder if he was trying to run us out of the house so this Goldlinger could get whatever it is he is after," Morgan said.

"Looks that way," Jolene answered.

"So these pirates have had us in their sights for quite some time," Celeste said, shivering as an icy finger tracing its way up her spine. She bit into her muffin, the warm softness filling her mouth with sweet flavor. She closed her eyes to savor it until a loud cracking sound from Fiona's side of the island made them fly open.

"What was that?" Morgan turned from the sink where she'd been washing the bowl.

Fiona stood at the island frowning down at her wrist. Celeste followed her gaze and saw one of the stones in her bracelet had shattered and was laying in pieces on the counter.

"Did you smash your bracelet on the counter?" she asked.

Fiona shook her head. "No. It just shattered on its own."

"That's weird," Morgan said. "I never heard of a stone doing that before."

"They don't, usually." Fiona picked up one of the shards and studied it under the light. "This stone is malachite. Ancient lore has it that the stone shatters to warn of impending danger.

Celeste's throat went dry, almost causing her to choke on the piece of muffin she'd just swallowed.

"No shit," Jolene said. "I'd say your stone is a little late with its warning."

As if on cue, spooky science fiction music erupted from Jolene's pocket and she pulled out her phone, slipping out of her chair and walking over to the other end of the kitchen to take the call.

Morgan, Celeste and Fiona bent over the shattered stone.

"It's probably just a coincidence." Morgan shrugged.

"Yeah, besides we already know we're in danger," Celeste said.

"Yeah, hopefully it's not a sign that things are going to get worse," Fiona added.

"It's not." Jolene rejoined them. "In fact things are starting to look up for us."

"Really?" Celeste's eyebrows flew up. "How so?"

"That was Skinner's brother. He wants to meet us over at Skinner's house. He said he has some of Skinner's notes and a poetry book that has to do with our case."

17

R einhardt Skinner's house was an old fashioned 1940s farmhouse that sat on a tree lined street. The four sisters parked across from it and approached from the front walkway.

"Does anyone else think it's strange that the door is open?" Celeste's stomach tightened as she pointed to the front door that was slightly ajar.

"Maybe he left it open to air out the house?" Jolene suggested. "He did say he was cleaning it out and it's been closed up for a few days.

"Maybe." Morgan's lips were pressed in a thin line. "But I have a feeling this might not be what we were hoping."

The girls walked toward the door cautiously. Jolene first, with Celeste, Morgan and Fiona close behind.

Jolene knocked on the door. "Mr. Skinner?"

No one answered.

Celeste's stomach tightened even more.

Jolene pushed the door open slightly, the hinge creaking like a sound effect from a bad horror movie.

"Hello?" Jolene said into the house.

No one answered.

Jolene looked back at Celeste. Celeste shrugged. Jolene turned back around, pushed the door wide and stepped into the house.

"Anyone home?" Jolene ventured.

Still no response.

She crept further into the house. Celeste, Morgan and Fiona came in behind her to stand in the small living room. The room was sparse with a sofa, television and recliner. An open can of soda sat on the coffee table and a few boxes were stacked in the corner. A bookshelf next to the sofa stood empty—evidence that Skinner's brother had already started packing. Dust motes floated in the air.

"Something's not right. He said he'd be here." Jolene turned to head down a hallway to the left when they heard a noise from the back of the house.

Celeste saw Morgan's eyes narrow as she put her finger up to her lips, cocking her ear in the direction of the noise.

Jolene wasn't as cautious as Morgan and she took off toward the back of the house.

"Jolene, no!" Morgan tried to grab for her but she was already out of reach, halfway through the dining room and closing in on the room the noise had come from.

Celeste sprinted up behind her and the two of them got to the opening that led into what must have been Skinner's study at the same time.

Celeste's heart jolted. Two beefy men with long scraggly hair and beards appeared to be ransacking the office. Desk drawers were pulled open, their contents spilled on the floor. The filing cabinet's oak drawers gaped and the bookshelf had been relieved of most of its books which now lay strewn in a heap. She knew they weren't looking for valuables—an expensive bronze bust sat untouched on top of an oak side table. But the most alarming sight was the body slumped over the desk in a pool of blood—Skinner's brother, Celeste assumed.

The two men's heads jerked up, their eyes narrowing at the sisters. Before Celeste could react, they threw down the papers they were holding and lunged toward her.

Celeste instinctively crouched into a defensive karate stance. Beside her she could see Jolene casting about for a weapon. Behind her, she could hear the sharp intake of breath as Morgan and Fiona joined them in time to see the two large men lunging in their direction.

She barely had time to register any of this when the largest of the men was practically on top of her. She thrust her palm out and up taking advantage of his forward momentum to maximize the impact of the heel of her palm to his nose. She heard a crunch and he jerked back, clutching his nose with a skull and cross bone tattooed hand while issuing a string of curses.

Beside her, the second man had tossed Jolene aside like she was a rag doll. Jolene teetered in the corner but Morgan and Fiona were on him—Morgan sending him stumbling with a jab of her elbow into his gut and Fiona jumping on his back. He spun this way and that, his arms flailing behind him, his bicep bulging and distorting the mermaid tattooed in the center as he tried to dislodge her.

The first man had recovered from the blow to his nose which was leaking blood and already starting to swell. From the look on his face, he was beyond mad. Panic clutched at Celeste's chest as she saw his huge hands reaching for her throat. She tried to back away but wasn't quick enough.

Her throat burned as he picked her up in the air, his hands squeezing. She could hear Jolene yelling at him to let go as her vision started to blur. Out of the corner of her eye she saw Jolene pick up a heavy paperweight from the desk and bash it into the side of the man's head.

He let go and turned on Jolene. Celeste dropped to the floor, sputtering and rubbing her neck. She saw Jolene put up her forearm to ward the guy off. Behind her, Celeste could see the guy with the mermaid tattoo had shaken Fiona off his back and was turning on her. Celeste's eyes grew wide as she saw the green stone pendant on Fiona's neck start to glow, softly at first and then brighter and brighter until it was almost pulsating. It must have surprised the attacker too because he was just standing there staring at the pendant when it exploded into pieces, one of which embedded itself in his eye.

Celeste felt the glow of satisfaction as the guy went down on one knee shrieking like a girl and holding his eye, blood seeping out from between his fingers. She didn't have long to revel in it though, because old skull and crossbones had Jolene by the hair and looked like he was about to smash her face into the wall.

Celeste looked around for something hard to hit him with.

Where was that paperweight?

Her hands fumbled for it as she kept one eye on Jolene who was squirming and twisting, somehow managing to wiggle around and bash the man across the face with her fist. A spark of electricity arced out of Jolene's hand and seared a jagged line into the man's skin. He jumped back, his hands flying protectively up to his face.

Celeste's fingers found a heavy vase and she raised it above her head, daring the men to come after her. Their injuries had slowed them down, but they still seemed hell bent on fighting with her and her sisters. Mermaid tattoo had stopped screaming was starting to advance on her when something in the corner by the closet caught her eye. A swirly white mist that looked an awful lot like Reinhardt Skinner. It seemed agitated, jumping up and down and pointing to the closet floor.

The distraction proved to be unfortunate. Mermaid tattoo rammed into her knocking her to the floor. She dropped the vase, shooting her arm out to break the fall and heard a sickening crunch as lightening hot pain shot up her arm.

She glanced over at Skinner's ghost who was still hopping up and down and pointing. He looked a little peeved that she wasn't paying enough attention to him. *Couldn't he see that she was kind of busy?*

Her heart crunched as the guy with the mermaid tattoo loomed above her. She tried to stand but with only one arm, all she managed to do was wobble around on the floor. Out of the corner of her eye, she could see the other guy recovering from being branded by Jolene—he was a mess with a bloody nose and shiny scar. Judging by the roar he gave out before he lunged at Jolene he must have been pissed.

Celeste sat there on the floor helplessly cradling her arm, leaning against the oak side table and watching as the man launched himself at her sister. She saw Jolene put her hand out to ward him off, then heard a sharp crackle like lightning and saw a bright light right before the bronze bust toppled off the side table, cracking her skull and turning everything black.

18

C eleste's head felt like it had been dumped inside a cement mixer and her eyelids seemed to be glued shut. Her throat burned, her tongue felt thick and dry. She tried to move, her skin rasping against crisp linen sheets.

A warm hand covered hers.

"Celeste?"

Was that Cal?

Her heart swelled and she struggled to open her eyes. She was surprised to discover how relieved she felt to hear his voice. She didn't realize how hurt she'd been when he'd left the night before without even saying good-bye. Which made her wonder if she'd made a mistake in pushing him away.

She was starting to realize she had feelings for him

that went beyond the friendship they'd shared for decades. That scared her—she'd learned early on never to depend on anyone but herself and her sisters. Even though Cal had always been there for her, he wasn't known for his long-term relationship skills. *Would getting involved with him only end up in her getting hurt and the end of their friendship?*

"You're okay. You're in the hospital." His voice ripped her out of her thoughts.

Hospital? Why would she be in the hospital?

Then the memory of the fight with the tattooed pirates came flooding back and she jerked her eyes open searching the room for her sisters.

"Are my sisters okay?" She bolted upright in the bed causing a wave of nausea and dizziness.

Cal pushed her back down. "They're fine. They just went to the cafeteria."

She accepted the cup of water he handed her, sucking it down in one gulp which made her throat burn a little less and her tongue return to its normal size. The headache, on the other hand, was probably going to require something stronger.

For the first time she noticed her lower arm was in a cast.

"What the heck?" She held it up raising her eyebrows at Cal.

"You broke your wrist and got a nasty bang on the

head. No concussion though, thankfully."

"Oh, I remember now."

"Your sisters told me you guys had quite a brawl."

Celeste laughed. "Yeah, I think we beat the crap out of those guys too."

The concern in Cal's eyes melted her heart. "Well, let's hope you guys don't make a habit out of it … even though some of you seem to have some special skills in that department."

Celeste chewed on her bottom lip remembering how Fiona's necklace had exploded and Jolene's strange power—talk about lightning reflexes.

Cal's phone made a dinging noise and he released her hand to answer it. From where she lay in the bed she could see the name of the caller—Camilla. Her heart sank. She never used to mind when girls called him before—her feelings were getting so complicated now.

"I have to take this." He stood and walked over to the window.

She felt a warm tingle as she studied his face silhouetted against the window. She'd always thought he was attractive in a brotherly sort of way … but now, what she was feeling was anything but sisterly.

He snapped the phone shut and came over to the bed. "I've got to go. I just wanted to stop in and make sure you were okay."

"Thanks for stopping by." She managed a weak smile.

"Okay, see you later." He turned and then disappeared out the door without even a peck on the cheek.

Celeste felt a hot poker stab her heart. He hadn't been his usual friendly self ... and now he was running off to see Camilla. Her gut wrenched. Had she made the biggest mistake of her life by pushing him away after he'd kissed her?

"You're up!" Fiona breezed into the room, a paper cup of coffee in her hand. "Are you in pain? You look upset."

"No." Celeste forced a smile. "I feel good. If you consider feeling like you drank a bottle of one-fifty-one, got run over by a dump truck and slept in a barn *good*."

Fiona laughed. "Well you did get a nasty bump ... You must have a whopper of a headache."

"Yeah. What happened back there?" Celeste smiled at Morgan and Jolene who joined them with their own paper cups. "And where's my coffee?"

"No coffee for you." Morgan handed her a bottle of orange juice. "You're recovering."

Celeste sipped the juice while she listened to her sisters recount what happened after she got knocked out. Apparently their attackers had been so freaked after the lightning bolt, they fled. Jolene had called 911, an ambulance came for Celeste and the police came for Skinner's brother. They did take the opportunity in between the bad guys leaving and the police arriving to search Skinner's office, but they didn't find anything ... which was weird because the pirates left empty handed.

"I'm surprised Overton didn't arrest one of you for the murder," Celeste said.

"Well, he did give us a hard time but it almost seemed like his heart wasn't in it," Morgan answered.

"He was probably too excited about giving the map to Goldlinger," Fiona whispered over the rim of her cup.

Celeste stared at the malachite shard hanging from her sister's necklace. Fiona's hand flew up to the shard and the sisters shared an uneasy look.

"That pendant was malachite, the same as the stone that shattered in your bracelet, right?" Celeste asked.

Fiona nodded.

"I'd be careful about wearing malachite if I were you," Jolene joked.

"Yeah, well I'll take your advice since I don't want to get on your bad side. I hear you pack an electrifying punch," Fiona replied.

The sisters laughed uneasily, then Celeste said, "Now I know what grandma meant the other day."

"What do you mean?" Morgan asked.

"She said that we, meaning the four of us." Celeste waved her good hand around the room, "were *stronger than we know* and that we had skills to fight the evil forces that were coming. I think she was referring to our special ... umm ... gifts."

"Yeah, *weird* gifts." Jolene looked at her hand. "I just wish I knew more about it and how to control it."

"Yeah, me too." Fiona fiddled with the broken pendant on her necklace. "I don't even know what my *gift* is."

"Well, you seem to have some power with crystals and gemstones. It's no wonder you chose to be a gemologist," Celeste said, then turned to Morgan. "Morgan has some kind of intuition ... we've seen it a couple of times now and Grandma even said for her to trust her gut instincts. Jolene has some sort of special energy and I talk to dead people. I guess we just need to focus on honing our skills, so to speak."

"The same as you would to develop any skill, like learning to be good at tennis or drawing?" Jolene asked.

"I think so." Morgan tossed her cup in the trash. "So far we've been ignoring our gifts or powers or whatever you want to call them. I guess it's time we started paying more attention and seeing how we can put them to good use."

"Speaking of which," Celeste pushed the sheets

aside and dangled her legs off the side of the bed, "I saw Skinner's ghost in that study when we were fighting those pirates. He seemed to be indicating that he wanted us to look at something on the bottom of the closet."

She slid her feet onto the floor, standing cautiously, holding onto the bed railings. Fiona rushed over and took her elbow to help steady her.

"Are you sure you should be getting out of bed?" Jolene's forehead wrinkled with concern.

"Sure, I only have a broken wrist. Besides I have to get out of here ASAP so we can get over to Skinner's and find what it was his ghost wants us to find."

"But how can we do that? His brother was murdered so I'm sure it's all closed off as a crime scene," Morgan said.

"Oh don't worry about that." Jolene's eyes sparkled. "I know just what we can do to get inside Skinner's house without the police ever knowing we were there."

* * *

CAL GLANCED BACK UP at the hospital as he walked across the parking lot. He'd *had* to come and see for himself that Celeste was okay. Folding himself into his car, he shoved the key in the ignition cursing the heavy weight dragging down his heart. He wasn't used to feeling this way.

He'd hated leaving without saying anything to Celeste the night before, but he'd been hurt when she'd pushed him away … which was strange because plenty of girls had turned him down and it never really bothered him before.

Why had he even kissed her in the first place? Celeste was his oldest and best friend. He'd known the Blackmoore sisters since they were kids. Even though they were all like sisters to him, he was closest to Celeste. Except lately, the way he felt about her had taken a whole different turn.

Last night, kissing her had seemed natural, he'd wanted to badly but, apparently she didn't feel the same way. For some reason, that crushed him. And Cal wasn't used to it. Most women were very receptive to his kisses, but with the few that hadn't he'd just shrugged and moved on.

He couldn't do that with Celeste though. She was more than just a casual fling. She was important. She mattered to him, probably more than any other person in his life.

He drove out of the parking lot, pulling in a deep breath as he glanced back at the hospital in his rear view mirror. Celeste had been a big part of his life since he was a boy. Anytime he had anything serious to discuss, he called Celeste. They'd celebrated all their life's high points … and commiserated the low points together. And they always had fun when they were together.

Why hadn't he recognized his feelings for her sooner? Maybe he just hadn't been ready until now. But the worst part was he didn't know if he could go back to just being friends with Celeste now that he knew what his true feelings for her were.

He pointed his car toward *The Bull and Claw* where he was meeting Camilla—not for a date like Camilla was probably hoping. He was going to break it off with her.

Cal could feel his care-free bachelor days coming to an end. Camilla was fun and all, but she wasn't anyone he'd want to spend the rest of his life with. Not like Celeste. Somehow he didn't have the heart for playing the field anymore—casual dating had lost its appeal.

His gut was telling him he should just forget about Celeste—steer clear of her and his feelings would subside. Out of sight, out of mind. Except he couldn't just abandon the Blackmoore's. They needed him to help decipher the journal. He *had* to help them. Hopefully he could do what needed to be done and keep his contact with Celeste to a minimum. He just hoped his heart would survive.

19

They waited three hours for the doctor to release Celeste and it was dark by the time they left the hospital. Jolene said that was perfect for what she had in mind, which might have made Celeste worry more if she hadn't been liberal with the pain pills.

The sisters tried to talk her into going straight home, but Celeste won the argument by telling them she was the only one that knew exactly where Skinner's ghost had been pointing.

Now, standing in the dark outside Skinner's back door while Jolene tried to pick the lock, Celeste questioned the wisdom of her ways.

"Are you sure you know what you're doing?" Morgan whispered.

"Shhh." Jolene fanned her hand behind her. "I've almost got it."

Celeste heard a click and then her heart skipped a beat as Jolene pushed the door open and slipped inside. Morgan, Fiona and Celeste followed.

Inside the house was dark. Moonlight filtered in through the windows causing eerie shadows. They stood in the kitchen for a few seconds listening to the silence. No ghosts appeared, although Celeste felt like this would be the perfect time for one to pop out from a wall and scare the crap out of her.

"The study's over here." Jolene took a small flashlight out of her jacket pocket, pointed the beam at the floor and started walking. Celeste and her sisters followed. The floor creaked and groaned under their feet, each sound sending Celeste's stomach plummeting.

They went through the dining room stopping short at the study door, which was taped off with yellow crime scene tape. Jolene hesitated but a second, then ducked under the tape lifting it for her sisters to follow.

Celeste's stomach roiled as she remembered the fight they'd had with the bad guys ... and how Skinner's brother's body had lain slumped on the desk the whole time. The blood stain was visible on the top of the desk and the room was still littered with papers.

The bronze bust that had cracked her head hadn't moved from where it had fallen on the floor.

"Okay, so where should we look?" Fiona raised her brows at Celeste.

"Over here." She crossed to the closet where she'd seen the ghost. The closet was empty and the door was open just as it had been during the fight. She stood in the doorway and looked into the closet but it was too dark to see anything.

"Shine the light down there." She indicated the bottom corner of the closet where Skinner's ghost had been pointing.

The beam of Jolene's flashlight shone on an empty space. Celeste's heart skipped—there was nothing there except the wide pine flooring and an old wire coat hanger.

"It's empty." Jolene looked up at Celeste. "Now what?"

"I don't know. Do you think Overton took whatever was there?"

Morgan shook her head. "I don't think they took anything. I was here most of the time the police were here—Overton only let Fiona go to the hospital with you. He made me and Jolene stay and give a statement."

"A statement? I imagine you left out a few details about the fight," Celeste said.

Morgan laughed. "Yeah, we only told them what they needed to know. They didn't take anything with them other than the body."

Celeste pressed her lips together. Her wrist was starting to throb and she wondered if Skinner had sent her on a wild goose chase.

Morgan came over to the closet door and squatted down motioning for Jolene to hand over the flashlight.

"You know how I have a secret hiding place in my room at home?" Morgan asked.

"The one you've had since you were a kid—that you refuse to tell us where it is?"

"Yep." Morgan straightened the hook on the wire coat hanger and scraped at the floor. "I bet Skinner had a similar hiding spot."

Celeste held her breath while Morgan wiggled the coat hanger around, then pushed it under the crack in one of the floorboards and pried part of the board up.

"See." She aimed the light of the flashlight inside the hole.

Celeste felt deflated. "It looks empty."

"Lemme see." Morgan fished around in the hole with her hand.

"Are you looking for this?" Celeste's heart jerked upon hearing the voice come from the other side of the room. They'd been so intent on watching Morgan, they hadn't noticed anyone approach.

"You!" Jolene spun around, shining the light on the man. A man Celeste recognized from an earlier mysterious encounter. Mateo. He was holding up the Poetry book—the key they needed to decipher the journal.

Jolene crossed the room in three angry steps and grabbed the book out of his hand. "Give me that!"

A startled look crossed his face. "I brought it here to give to you."

"Yeah, sure" Jolene narrowed her eyes at him. "Then why are you sneaking around here in the middle of the night?"

"Why are you?"

"I … well …" Jolene looked around at her sisters. "None of your business, that's why."

Mateo's laugh had a deep, pleasing timbre to it and his smile seemed genuine. Celeste noticed he was handsome in a dark, exotic kind of way. She also noticed that he was looking at Jolene with quite a bit of interest.

Jolene must have noticed too because she backed away from him, holding the book against her chest.

"What do you want?" Morgan asked.

Mateo shrugged, holding his hands out at his sides. "Nothing. I *am* here to help you … sort of."

"Help us how?"

"I can't really say much more. But I took the book from the closet … to keep it from your enemies and now I must go. We shouldn't be seen together." He turned and slipped out of the room.

"Wait! You can't just run off ..." Jolene ran out of the room after him.

Morgan replaced the floor board and dusted off her hands. "Well, looks like we got what we came for."

Jolene returned into the room. "He disappeared. Can you believe that guy?"

"It does seem odd, but I'm not going to complain. That book is the final piece of the puzzle we need to figure out where the treasure is," Celeste said cradling her bad arm against her chest. The pain was starting to escalate and she was getting to the point where she cared more about taking a pain pill and going to bed than she did about fending off pirates or finding a treasure.

"Is your wrist starting to hurt?" Fiona asked. "When we get home I'll find a carnelian that you can wrap up next to the cast. That should help it heal."

Celeste remembered that carnelian was a healing stone. Fiona had given one to Jolene when she'd cut her arm and it had healed it overnight. Celeste was skeptical about it healing her broken wrist but she'd try just about anything right now.

"We should get you home now." Morgan started toward the door.

"But we don't know if the book is what Skinner's ghost wanted us to find." Jolene glanced over at the closet.

"The closet's empty so even if it isn't what he wanted, there's no reason for us to stay. Plus we need to get cracking on that journal now that we have the cipher key," Fiona said.

"But we still don't even know if Mateo is a good guy or a bad guy." Jolene glanced toward the door.

"Well how could he possibly be a bad guy? He gave us the book," Morgan replied.

Jolene looked suspiciously at the book. "Maybe it's a fake. To throw us off track like we did to Overton."

Morgan held her hand out and Jolene put the book in it. Morgan thumbed the pages holding them under the beam from the flashlight. "It looks authentic to me. It would be hard to fake an old book like this. Besides, I'm getting good vibes from it. Mateo *is* on our side."

Jolene sighed. "But he's so … mysterious," she sputtered.

"And cute," Morgan added as she made her way toward the door.

Jolene rolled her eyes and they all followed Morgan out. Celeste looked back into the room as she crossed the threshold and saw two swirls of mist over by the closet. Skinner and his brother? One of them gave her a thumbs up and then they both disappeared, leaving her with a warm feeling around her heart knowing the book *was* what Skinner wanted her to find *and* that the two brothers were together ... wherever they were.

20

Celeste rolled over in her bed, startling herself as the cast on her hand banged hollowly into the headboard. She'd forgotten about her wrist.

She moved her arm tentatively, surprised to discover it didn't hurt at all. Pushing herself to a sitting position, she leaned back against the pillows she had piled at the head of the bed and peeked at the orange carnelian stone Fiona had slipped into the edge of the cast. *Guess it must be doing the trick.*

Since there were no ghosts or cats to distract her, she got out of bed and slipped on a pair of sweatpants and a sweatshirt. The early fall Maine nights were growing chilly which meant for chilly mornings—by noon she'd be changing back into Capri's and a tee-shirt.

Her head still throbbed with a dull pain but it was much milder than the day before. She did have a tender spot on the back and brushing her hair didn't appeal to her so she simply ruffled it with her fingers and headed downstairs.

In the kitchen, Celeste found a note from Morgan under a packet of herbs. Her heart warmed, knowing her sister had made a special concoction of willow bark and chamomile for her to steep into a tea which would help her headache. She heated some water, grabbed a mug and dunked the teabag, watching the steam waft up.

Voices drifted out from the informal living room so she headed in that direction. Standing in the doorway, she could see Jolene and Cal sitting next to each other on the sofa, their heads bent over the coffee table. Cal looked up and her heart skipped when their eyes met.

"Morning." She cracked a smile, walking further into the room.

"Hey Sis, how are you feeling?" Jolene asked.

"Pretty good." Celeste held up her bad arm. "My wrist doesn't even hurt at all. I guess those gemstones really do work."

"Don't I know it," Jolene said looking at the fading scar on her own arm.

"So what are you guys doing?" Celeste perched on

the edge of one of the overstuffed chairs and leaned forward for a better look.

The old journal and the poetry book both lay spread open on the table. Cal had a notebook in front of him and it appeared they were attempting to decipher the book. Her heart tugged when she remembered her and Cal doing a similar exercise earlier in the summer, their heads bent together over those very same books. But that was before she screwed things up.

"Jake brought the journal back so we're trying to decipher this thing and figure out what Skinner found," Cal said, keeping his eyes glued firmly to the books.

"Any luck?"

Jolene puffed out her cheeks. "Not really. The journal is pretty big and we have no idea exactly *where* Skinner made his find."

"And we're running out of time," Cal added. "The low tide is tomorrow night, which means we only have about 30 hours to figure out where this treasure is so we can take it away from the pirates."

"Yeah, and I keep looking over my shoulder thinking they are going to come for us."

Celeste rolled the mug in her palms. It was warm and soothing but she still felt panic starting to claw at her gut. What if the pirates broke in like they did earlier in the summer? How would they manage to fight them off *and* figure out the clue in the journal? And what if one of them got kidnapped again?

"Where's Morgan and Fiona?"

"They had some customer orders to tend to so they went to *Sticks and Stones*. Luke sent Buzz with them just in case."

"Okay, well how can I help?" Celeste put her mug down on a side table and slid down onto the floor next to the coffee table, ready to help with the journal.

Jolene looked at her watch. "Actually, I have to go meet Jake. You can take over scanning the journal for passages that might be of interest. I've been finding them and Cal's been looking up the code in the poetry book."

Jolene slid the journal around so that it was facing Celeste then stood up and started toward the front hall.

Cal looked up from the book. "See you later."

Jolene smiled in his direction. "No problem. Good luck you guys."

"Thanks," Celeste said as she watched her disappear. A few seconds later, she heard the front door click open, then shut again, announcing Jolene's departure.

She and Cal were alone in the house ... like they had been many times before, except this time it felt incredibly awkward. Celeste decided the best course was to focus on finding what they needed from the journal.

"She was looking back to front," Cal said, flipping a page of the journal and pointing. "Here's where she stopped."

"Okay, thanks." Celeste murmured as she studied the page. The paper itself was yellowed and brittle. She was almost afraid to turn the pages for fear of them disintegrating. The scrolly writing, done with some sort of quill or fountain pen was faded and marred with dots of ink. The paragraphs were long and didn't make much sense as they were encoded.

"I feel like we should be looking for a poem or a riddle or something. Remember how the clues we found earlier were poems?" She looked up at Cal.

"I think you're right." He looked up and their eyes met, causing a riot of emotions to run through her. Glancing back down at his book just as quickly he added, "Maybe we should focus on only the pages where the text is broken up into centered lines, like a poem would be."

"Good idea." Celeste flipped the pages carefully while Cal worked on deciphering the last passage he and Jolene had thought worthwhile.

He sighed, put the pen down and rubbed his face with his hands. "This one doesn't give us any clue. It talks about some silks and silver he brought back from the West Indies. It mentions his exotic bride. Was his wife from the West Indies?"

Celeste's forehead puckered. "I have no idea. That's kind of interesting actually—I'd like to dig into that some more, but right now, I have a passage here that might be what we are looking for."

She turned the book to face him and pointed to a section of text that consisted of two uneven rows, situated in the center of the book. He copied each word down on a separate piece of paper, then started flipping the poetry book open to the various passages and scribbling down each word as he figure them out.

Celeste took the journal back and continued looking in case the poem was a dead end.

"This is interesting." Cal tapped the end of the pen on the table as he studied the translated poem."

"What?" Celeste cocked her head sideways and Cal slid the paper in her direction so she could read it.

A treacherous maze
Two maps are better then one
The hide marks the spot

"WHAT'S THAT MEAN?" She wrinkled her face at him.

Cal pressed his lips together "I'm not sure but I

think that last line might refer to the map we found this summer ... the one that was on leather—or *hide*."

Celeste glanced over at the table. The ornate silver box was back in place. Jake must have brought it when he returned the journal. She got up from her seat and crossed to the box, then opened it. A leather treasure map was rolled up neatly inside as was the maze map that Jolene had found in her pocket. She lifted out the leather map and brought it over to the coffee table spreading it out awkwardly, the cast on her wrist interfering with her normal movement.

"Here, let me help." Cal pushed the journal aside to make room for the map which he spread out facing him. "Do you have that map of the maze handy?"

"Yep, it was right in the box." She turned and grabbed it, handing it to Cal.

He placed it on the table, just above the leather map. Resting his chin in his hand he studied them. Celeste looked at them from a right angle—she didn't see anything that might be helpful.

"Look at this." Cal pointed to a spot on the map and Celeste tilted her neck to see it from the same angle as him.

"I don't see anything."

"Come over here and you'll get a better look." He motioned to the couch beside him and Celeste's stomach did a little flip as she walked over and slid onto the sofa. She leaned forward, her eyes flicking between the two maps. The shape did look sort of similar, but she had no idea what it meant.

"See how the leather map has the same sort of boundary shapes as the middle of the maze map?" Cal asked.

"Yes."

"Well, I wonder if the maze map shows you how to get to where the treasure is and the leather map shows you the final step of how to dig it up or something."

Celeste squinted at the maps. "It could, but this whole time I thought the leather map was a map of the area of tunnels that blew up this summer. That's where all the clues led us."

"Yeah me too, but what if it wasn't? What if the tunnels were just a decoy and this whole time the clues have been leading us to somewhere else ... where the real treasure is?"

"It could be. But look at the leather map. It looks like the edges show the ocean outside where the treasure is ... but everything else we've found seems to indicate the treasure is *in* the ocean." She leaned forward to point at the crude waves drawn on the edges of the map and her knee brushed against Cal's sending sparks shooting through her.

She glanced over and he was looking at her the same way she was looking at him. He'd felt it too.

Time slowed down. She was aware of the muted cry of seagulls outside on the ocean, the dust motes hanging in the slats of sun that filtered in the window and Cal's sapphire eyes drilling into hers. A warm tingle of attraction clutched at her belly as Cal slowly leaned toward her.

Would he kiss her again?

She certainly hoped so … and this time she had no intention of pushing him away.

And then his cell phone chirped.

Cal jerked back on the couch and dug in his pocket, pulling out the offending gadget and looking at the display.

"Oh, sorry, I have an appointment. I have to go." He stood up, backing away from the couch … and her. "If you can pick out any more passages which look promising, that would be great. I'll be back later tonight to help decipher them."

Then he turned and practically ran out of the room before she could even say good-bye.

21

She certainly didn't need Cal Reed to help her decipher an old journal, Celeste thought, as she leafed through the old book looking for poem shaped passages. Surely she and her sisters could figure out how to lookup the code. It seemed simple enough.

Two hours later, she hadn't found one other poem-like entry when Fiona and Morgan came home.

"How's your wrist?" Fiona sat beside her, holding out her hand for Celeste's cast wrapped wrist.

"It's pretty good. Actually it doesn't even hurt at all." She submitted to Fiona's tapping and poking. Fiona slid a ruby nailed finger into the gap between the palm of her hand and the cast and pulled the carnelian out.

"So this did the trick, then?"

"I think so. I don't know if it's healed but it doesn't hurt anymore."

"Oh, it's probably all healed by now. You should go back to the doctor and have that thing removed.

Celeste rolled her eyes. "Yeah, I can picture the look on his face when I tell him my sister put a rock in the cast and I'm certain it must have healed my broken wrist."

Fiona and Morgan laughed.

"Well, maybe you *should* wait the appropriate amount of time just to save from having to explain," Morgan suggested.

"So what's going on? Where's Cal? I thought he and Jolene were deciphering the journal." Fiona sat down next to Celeste to look at the items spread on the table.

"They were. But they both had to leave so I figured I might as well give it a go."

"Did you find anything?" Morgan asked.

"Earlier, when Cal was here, we deciphered this strange poem." Celeste pointed to the poem he had written down on a piece of paper. "Cal was wondering if the 'two maps' part might mean that there was another map and thought the leather map would be a good candidate because hide is another word for leather."

"So how do you use two maps to get to a treasure?" Fiona asked.

Celeste explained Cal's theory of one map showing the way through the maze and the other being the directions to where the treasure is buried.

Morgan stood beside the coffee table, frowning down at the poem. "Treacherous maze? That's ominous. What do you think makes the maze treacherous?"

Celeste shrugged. "Who knows?"

"This is all great and everything," Fiona said. "But it still doesn't tell us *where* the maze is."

Celeste puffed out her cheeks. "I know. And there's no other passages that look like poems. We're going to have to go through the whole book until we hit the part that tells where the maze is."

Morgan reached down and thumbed the pages. "It's a pretty big book. What if the part we need isn't obvious? I'm sure it doesn't come right out and say 'the maze with the treasure in it is located twenty degrees east of the opening to the channel' or anything like that."

"Well we have to do *something*," Celeste said. "The low tide is tomorrow night."

"Right, I'm beginning to think we should just wait for the pirates and then follow them," Fiona suggested.

"Luke said he got the geological map of the area and didn't see anything that looked like it would be exposed by the low tide," Morgan said. "But he did say one thing was odd—someone else had requested a geological map of the same exact area."

"The pirates?"

"Maybe." Morgan shrugged. "And now that Overton is going to give them the map, they'll know where the maze is and *think* they know how to navigate it to get to the treasure."

"So there's no need for them to come after us."

"Maybe, maybe not. Either way I don't want them taking our treasure … not after everything we've been through."

"Me either," Celeste said. "So we only have two choices … follow them or figure out where it is ourselves."

"And since we really don't have much else to do, we might as well work on figuring it out," Fiona said pulling the journal over to her side of the table.

The girls worked on the journal in silence each taking turns reading the words while another person flipped around in the poetry book to decode the word. After several hours, Celeste's headache was back and they'd only come up with mundane accounts of daily life as a 1700s sailor.

"Hey, where do you think the map of the maze came from anyway?" Morgan looked up from the poetry book. "I mean, I know Mateo put it in Jolene's pocket but where did *he* get it from?"

"I assume from Skinner or his office." Fiona shrugged.

"Okay, so then where did Skinner get it from? There's no drawing of a maze in the journal."

Fiona pulled the maze drawing in front of her on the table. "Well it's not an old drawing, so it's either a copy of an old drawing that someone drew themselves or, maybe the journal describes the map and Skinner drew it according to the instructions."

"Or Mateo got it through some other source," Celeste offered.

Morgan pressed her lips together. "Maybe we should be looking in the journal for something that is more like instructions or directions. If Isaiah Blackmoore wrote down instructions on how to draw the map, he probably would have something about where the maze is located near them."

"Good idea," Fiona agreed.

Celeste thought it was a good idea too, but her head was pounding and her eyelids grew heavy. She stifled a yawn. "I'm really beat. I might go lay down."

"You should." Fiona raised concerned eyes at her. "You're still recovering from that bash on the head. You need a lot of rest."

"Yeah and you'll need to be in tip top shape for tomorrow," Morgan added causing Celeste's stomach to crunch.

"Right, to fight off pirates and recover treasure," Celeste said. "Cal said he was coming back, but that was hours ago so I don't know if he's going to show or not."

"Where did he go?"

"He said he had a meeting," Celeste answered. Probably with Camilla, she thought to herself then felt an uncustomary surge of anger—he couldn't even hurry back for something this important? The anger was immediately replaced by guilt. It was her own fault he was with Camilla and not with her. Suddenly she felt very weary, she was overtired and needed to go to bed. Maybe tomorrow this wouldn't bother her so much.

"Okay, well, I'm heading off to bed." She got up from the sofa and shuffled out of the room.

"Take some Tylenol PM so you get a good rest," Morgan called after her.

Good idea. She veered into the kitchen and grabbed a couple of pills from the drawer. Glancing out the window at the ocean she felt herself shiver. After tomorrow night, things might never be the same.

22

S heriff Dwight Overton studied the map he'd taken from the Blackmoore residence.

"Those Blackmoore bimbo's didn't pick a very good hiding spot," he said into the empty room, congratulating himself on his cleverness.

He bent over his rickety kitchen table, squinting in the low light from the forty five watt bulb that hung overhead. His small apartment contained only the bare necessities—Noquitt was merely a temporary stop in his grand plan, so he hadn't bothered to spend any time or money on furnishings. It wouldn't be long before he was out of here and living in more luxurious accommodations.

The floorboards creaked as he crossed to the kitchen

drawer. He pulled it open rummaging inside for a pen that matched the ink on the map exactly. He sat down at the table and set about drawing a replica of the map —almost an exact replica except for a few key changes … like the directions on how to navigate through the maze.

He carefully traced the outline, his tongue sticking out of the side of his mouth, his hand shaking just slightly. He omitted some of the actual dead-ends and put in a few of his own before drawing the path that indicated which way to go to get to the treasure. The path he drew wasn't the same as the path on the map he had, of course, it was almost the exact opposite.

He finished the final line with a flourish and leaned back in the simple wooden chair he'd picked up for a buck at a yard sale, a smile spreading across his face. He didn't smile often, but this was cause for celebration—his years of hard work were finally about to pay off.

He folded the map carefully and put it in a plain white envelope inside a paper bag. Later on tonight, he'd drop it off at the designated spot where one of Goldlinger's lackeys would pick it up. The thought of Goldlinger made his bowels cramp. Overton shuddered to think what the man would do to him if he found out the map was a fake.

But Overton was smart. He'd planned things to the letter. By the time Goldlinger figured out he'd been double-crossed. Overton would be miles away, using a different name. Plus, if he was lucky, the Blackmoore's and that meddling Luke Hunter would have taken care of most of Goldlinger's henchmen for him and weakened Goldlinger's operation so he'd have no resources left to chase Overton.

His smile turned into a smirk as he thought about the lucky break he'd gotten when Goldlinger sent him here to investigate the death of the Blackmoore girl's mother. To *make sure* it was ruled a suicide. Goldlinger had pulled a lot of strings to get Overton in place there and he'd known there was more to it than just fixing a death investigation.

It had taken four long years to get to this point. Even though the small town Sheriff's position was boring and demeaning, there had been some things he'd enjoyed. Like putting the screws to the Blackmoore sisters.

He'd hated the Blackmoore's on sight and delighted in making them miserable. Serving them with trumped up citations, finagling evidence and paying off judges so he could throw them in jail. In fact, he would have loved to have thrown a couple of them in jail for Skinner's murder, but he didn't have the time to rig up the evidence. He had much more important things to focus on now.

Overton folded the real map and put it in his top shirt pocket. He'd keep it close where no one could take it from him. He wanted to know exactly where it was because it was critical he have it on hand tomorrow night when the tide was its lowest.

He turned around and reached out to open the drawer of a small side table he had against the wall. His heartbeat quickened with excitement as he pulled out a piece of paper and spread it out on the table.

The paper was a geographical contour map of Noquitt which showed a specific spot. A spot that Overton was sure Goldlinger didn't know about. A secret tunnel of sorts that opened just at the channel that led into Perkins Cove. It was covered by water now, but during the lowest tide, he'd be able to gain access.

According to his calculations, he'd be able to start his journey toward the maze about two hours before dead tide. That would give him an hour to get in, grab all the treasure he could and get out before the ebb tide submerged the treasure for another three hundred years.

And all the while, Goldlinger's men would be wandering around lost in the maze.

Overton laughed out loud as he shoved himself

away from the table. Grabbing his sheriff's hat, he shoved it on his head and started on the way to his mundane job at the police station for the last time ever.

After years of patiently waiting, he was finally going to get exactly what he deserved.

23

T *hirteen hours until dead tide.*

CELESTE HAD STARED at the journal for so long that it felt like an image of the pages would be burned into her retinas. Disappointment pressed on her like a weight—only thirteen hours until dead tide and they still had no idea where the maze was.

She looked out the window at the Atlantic. The first low tide of the day would be in about a half hour, just shortly before noon. But that wouldn't be the *lowest* tide of the day. That tide would come tonight. … at almost exactly midnight, the water would be at the very lowest point—dead tide.

Luke and his men were still out on the ocean today watching, even though they all agreed that the pirates would probably make their move at night, under the cover of darkness. They figured the pirates would make their way into the maze—wherever *that* was—shortly before midnight so they could be in place when dead tide hit. They might only have a short period of time to recover the treasure before the tide started to come back in.

Celeste could feel the tension in her shoulders. Maybe if she could figure out what the significance of low tide was, she could figure out where the maze was. Frustration gnawed at her. She had no idea where to start looking—now would be a good time for her grandmother to appear and give her some sort of clue, but she hadn't.

"The tide *really* is a lot lower than I've ever seen it." Jolene had come into the room and was standing next to her at the window, pointing at the rocks that stood out from the ocean.

"Yeah, that rock there is usually only jutting out of the water at the very top. Now you can see a whole crop of rocks below it."

"But no maze, huh?" Morgan said from the other side of the room. Celeste turned and her stomach grumbled at the tray of grapes, cheese and crackers Morgan had in her hand. Fiona came in with a pitcher of lemonade and they all sat down on the overstuffed chairs being careful not to get the food or drinks near the journal.

Celeste noticed Fiona was wearing a new necklace in place of the malachite one that had exploded. This one was a big blue stone—the aquamarine she and Cal had found in the attic.

Fiona caught her looking and her hand flew up to the stone. "I figured I'd wear it since my other one shattered and … well, it seems appropriate. You guys don't mind do you?"

"Of course not," Celeste answered for all of them. "Though with the way the malachite one helped us beat those pirates, maybe you should be wearing another one of those."

Fiona laughed. "I should have made one for all of us. I did, however, bring that satchel of crystals we found in the attic last summer."

She pointed to a burlap bag that was laying on the floor. Celeste recognized it as one they had found in the attic during the big treasure hunt in the summer. It had the initials MB on it which they thought might stand for Mariah Blackmoore, the wife of Isaiah Blackmoore.

The sack contained a variety of large crystals. The girls found it interesting that an ancestor apparently had the same affinity for them as Fiona.

"Why did you bring those?" Celeste's brows mashed together as she opened the flap to look inside.

"Morgan told me to. She had a feeling." Fiona looked at Morgan. "And we all know we should pay attention to those now."

Belladonna appeared out of nowhere and eyed the cheese expectantly. Celeste broke off a small piece, offering it to the cat who sniffed it daintily for two full minutes before taking it.

"So what do we do now?" Jolene asked.

"We finish deciphering the book," Fiona answered.

"Cal was here until dawn and we made it through a lot of the book," Jolene said, layering a slice of cheese on top of a saltine and crunching into it. "But we didn't find any clues about the maze, yet."

"He went home to catch up on some sleep. He's supposed to be here soon. Until then we can still make progress ourselves." Morgan popped a grape into her mouth.

Celeste caught herself wondering *whose* home Cal went to.

"I just feel so useless sitting here. Shouldn't we be out there doing something." Jolene gestured toward the window.

"Well Luke's men are on the ocean looking for the pirates to come by sea. Luke's taking the evening shift and will be out there himself tonight," Morgan said.

"And more of Luke's guys are watching the house along with Jake just in case the pirates come here."

An icy finger traced Celeste's spine. It seems odd that pirates hadn't made a move at them but then again if they have the map, they might think they have everything and not even bother with the girls. Still she couldn't help but feel it was the calm before the storm.

"So, Luke's out on the water, Jake's watching the house and we're supposed to sit here and do what?" The tone in Celeste's voice showed her frustration.

"Hopefully find the answer to where the maze is," Jolene said. "Because I don't know about you, but I'm gonna be pissed if the pirates make off with a treasure that belongs to us!"

"Meow!" Belladonna jumped up onto Jolene's lap as if to say she agreed.

Celeste rubbed her eyes and pulled the journal over toward her, steeling herself for a long afternoon of deciphering. "Okay, I guess we might as well get started. Which page did you leave off on?"

24

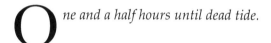

O ne and a half hours until dead tide.

DWIGHT OVERTON silently paddled the wooden dinghy from the dock in Perkins Cove toward the end of the channel. He wore a dark shirt and pants hoping that no one would notice him gliding slowly under the bridge toward the mouth of the cove. Not that anyone was around to see him—it was past ten p.m. and the cove was basically shut down for the night.

The water glittered in the moonlight as it quietly lapped the edges of the cove. The rocks that had been built up to form the sides of the channel revealed how low the tide really was. There was a clear line where the water normally leveled off and now it was a good ten feet below that. Overton knew it would get even lower in the hours to come, but he wanted to get a head start. He'd need some time to locate the entrance. Glancing back in the boat behind him he double checked his supplies one last time. A shovel, buckets and a wheeled dolly—everything he needed.

The paddling was easy since the current did most of the work. As he neared the mouth of the channel, Overton took out the geological map. He'd marked it with longitude and latitude coordinates of the slight anomaly in the channel floor that he'd seen. Most people wouldn't have noticed, but Overton knew this anomaly wasn't natural, something man-made was there and he had a good idea who made it—the old pirate Isaiah Blackmoore.

Glancing at his GPS watch, his heartbeat sped up as he checked his location. If his hunch was correct, the entrance to the maze was just to his left. He used the paddle to steer the dinghy to the side which gradually sloped downwards toward the water, giving him a convenient place to park.

He hopped out of the boat into water that was up to his knees. His breath rasped into his lungs as the frigid chill slapped him. His neoprene boot clad feet were almost instantly numb but he managed to shake off the cold and pull the boat up onto the side. He'd need it for his getaway later on.

Hitching up his pants, he turned his attention to the rock covered slope and searched for the indentation that he knew would be there. His heart kicked when he saw it right in front of him.

He grabbed the shovel and started moving the rocks away. His shoulders ached with the strain of the heavy boulders. He wasn't used to this type of physical labor but his excitement kept him going. Especially when he saw the gaping hole the rocks revealed … the mouth of the passage into the maze.

He quickly moved aside enough of the boulders to fit himself and his dolly inside, then he disappeared into the darkness of the tunnel.

25

F *ifty five minutes until dead tide.*

CELESTE LEANED BACK on the couch stretching her arms up over her head, her neck cracking loudly at the effort. She glanced at the clock, her skin prickling with nerves. It was less than one hour until dead tide and they still hadn't discovered where the treasure was.

"Who's hungry?" Jolene lay stretched out on her back on the other side of the informal living room. Belladonna was curled up on her stomach, the cat rising up and down every time Jolene took a breath.

"I am," Morgan answered.

"Me too," Fiona said.

"Ditto." Cal looked up from the journal with a sigh.

Celeste rubbed her stomach. Despite her nerves, she did feel a little hungry. "I could go for pizza."

Jolene rolled over, dislodging Belladonna who protested with an angry meow. She grabbed her cell phone from the table. "I have *Gino's Pizza* on speed dial. What do you guys want?"

They decided on a large pepperoni. Jolene made the order and they all leaned back in their chairs to take a break from the journal.

"Is anyone else getting worried that we haven't figure out where the maze is yet? I mean, it's less than an hour until the tide is its lowest," Fiona said.

Celeste looked over at her. *Was the very bottom of her aquamarine pendant glowing?* Must just be a reflection from the bright, full moon.

"It's frustrating," Morgan said. "I think we should come up with a plan B."

"I don't know about a plan B, but one of us has to go pick up the pizza," Jolene said.

"I'll go," Cal volunteered. "I could use the down time to try to figure out what the tie in is between the two maps. I feel like that could be a significant piece of the puzzle."

He got up from the chair he was sitting in, waved off an offer of money from Morgan and disappeared down the hall. Celeste's heart sank—he hadn't even looked over at her as he walked away.

"This journal deciphering is back breaking work." Fiona stood and stretched out her back.

"It sure is. And straining to make out the writing is killing my eyes," Morgan added.

"Especially with Belladonna sticking her face into the book all day," Jolene said petting the cat affectionately.

Celeste felt the corners of her lips tug upwards in a smile. The cat had been a little disruptive all day, sticking her face in the journal as if she was trying to turn the pages. They'd had to shoo her away a few times because she'd caused them to lose their place in the book. Still it was kind of cute that she wanted to be a part of it.

"We've been at this all day and we haven't made any progress." Celeste looked out the picture window toward the ocean. *Were the pirates out there waiting to attack or would they just slip in, take the treasure and leave?* She stared at the black ocean. Usually the light from the full moon reflecting off the tops of the waves was a calming scene. But tonight she knew what might happen out there would be anything but calm.

"That's why I think we need another plan. We should prepare to meet these pirates head on. Let's let them lead us to the treasure and then we'll take it from them," Morgan said.

Fiona's forehead wrinkled. "How would we battle a bunch of killer pirates?"

"Well, we've done it before," Jolene pointed out.

Celeste shrugged. "Sure, maybe if our skills were more refined. But even then, if we tried that, Luke would have his men returning us to 'safety' before we even set foot out of the house."

"Yeah and Jake's out watching the house making sure no one breaks in too," Fiona said. "I'm sure he'd take a dim view of us seeking out the pirates."

"It's frustrating to sit here and wait for something to happen." Morgan paced the room, gnawing on a nail, Belladonna following back and forth at her heels.

"Or for the pizza to show up," Jolene joked.

Celeste picked up the poetry book. The book was the key to deciphering the journal, but it was also just a regular book. She wondered why Isaiah Blackmoore had chosen it as the cypher key.

Thumbing through the old book, she breathed in the musty smell of old paper. She'd always like that smell for some reason. The pages were brittle, and she thumbed them carefully, stopping to look at some of the black and white illustrations on the pages.

"Hey, let's take a break and read some of these

poems while we're waiting for the pizza. Just for fun," Jolene said.

Celeste shrugged, opening the book to the first page. "Sure, why not."

Fiona sat down opposite Celeste and Celeste couldn't help but notice the aquamarine pendant. It *was* glowing—just at the very bottom—and if her mind wasn't playing tricks on her, the glow was getting brighter.

26

F *ifty minutes until dead tide.*

OVERTON SLOSHED through the knee-high water, his breath coming in ragged gasps from the exertion. He could hardly feel his feet anymore—the water was like ice. Once the tide receded fully, the entire tunnel would be dry, but he wanted to get to the treasure as quickly as possible to ensure he could get out before the incoming tide filled the tunnel entirely and trapped him inside, sentencing him to a watery death.

He stumbled ahead on wooden feet, pulling the dolly under the water awkwardly behind him. The sharp, salty smell of the sea permeated his nostrils. The tunnel was dank and slimy. He slipped a few times but that didn't deter him from his quest.

His flashlight illuminated garlands of seaweed and starfish that clung to the tunnel walls. Flashing it ahead of him, his heart jerked when he saw a solid wall. He could go either left or right. *Which way?*

He took the map from his top pocket where he'd stored it in a ziplock bag so it wouldn't get wet. Drying his fingers thoroughly, he removed the paper from the bag and studied it.

He *thought* he was at the west entrance. But if he was, there should be no wall here. He turned the map one hundred eighty degrees and found it matched where he was better. The map indicated to go to the left, which he did.

Another ten or twenty feet and he felt the water level getting lower with each step. He didn't think it was the tide—too drastic of a drop for that. It felt like he was going uphill. He frowned down at the map. Shouldn't he be going downhill below sea level?

According to the map he should go straight, turn left through an opening a little ways up, and then left again. He followed it obediently, except there was no second left—he could only go right after the opening. Overton felt seeds of doubt take root in his belly. Was the map even right? Maybe he had taken a wrong turn?

He studied the map, turning it this way and that, trying to make out exactly where he was. He couldn't be lost—he'd planned everything so carefully—getting lost inside this dark, smelly maze was not an option. He shrugged and continued forward since it was the only path to take. Surely, the maze couldn't be so complicated that he couldn't figure out how to navigate it to the treasure?

Dragging the dolly forward he felt a spark of hope when he noticed the path was getting wider. He quickened his pace. He was nearly there … he could *feel* it.

The floor of the maze was damp with shallow puddles here and there. Overton could hear his boots crunching on the few unfortunate snails that had clung onto the rock floor instead of going out with the tide.

He turned into a narrow opening in the wall. He was going on instinct now, not even following the map, but he felt like he was heading in the right direction. His breath caught in his throat when he saw the remnants of what he was seeking—a sea chest lay open against the wall. It was empty, its edges sagging, the wood rotted from years of exposure but proof nonetheless that the treasure was near.

Shining the light in the passage ahead of him, his heart leapt when he saw a gaping hole in the passage floor in front of him. He crossed to the edge, shining his flashlight down into what looked like a black, bottomless pit. Two weathered boards lay next to each other as a bridge to cross to the other side. Overton eyed them dubiously but then his flashlight caught several glints of light from the other side of the path. He angled the flashlight, craning his neck to see what it was.

Gold coins!

He rushed on ahead, his skepticism about the sturdiness of the boards overruled by his greed. The old boards groaned as he stepped on them, causing his heart to twist. The gap was only about four feet and Overton figured he could make it in two or three long steps. He stretched out his right leg and placed it further on the board, his heart stopping when the board bowed under his weight. It held. He put his full weight on the right foot, lifting the left and moving it along the left board. That board bowed too, but he was almost to the other side. He lifted his right leg to repeat the process.

Snap!

The board gave way and Overton felt the sickening sensation of weightlessness before he fell. His arms grappled out by instinct catching on the other board and stopping him short with an abrupt jerk that practically pulled his arms out of the sockets.

The flashlight, which he had dropped, had miraculously landed on the board. It cast an eerie light on the passage. Fear clutched at his chest as he looked down at his legs dangling in the open space below. Sweat dripped from his brow.

He struggled to lift himself up onto the one remaining board but his weight was too much for him. He looked around the passage, his stomach sinking when he realized the only other people down here would be Goldlinger's men. If they found him down here, they'd know he was trying to get the treasure for himself and *that* would mean certain death.

27

F*orty five minutes until dead tide.*

BELLADONNA FLICKED her tail against the coffee table trying to draw attention to the two maps that lay spread on the surface but the sisters paid no attention to her, preferring to oooh and aaah at the sappy love poems in the old poetry book.

She sighed in exasperation, flopped down on her belly and licked the inside of her paw. Sometimes it was so hard to get through to the humans. She wondered why she even bothered. She'd spent most of the day trying to point out the very page in the journal they should look at. But they'd paid no attention, even going so far as to shoo her away!

She felt the hairs on her back prickle and sat upright, becoming alert to the energy in the house. Something was happening below … something that needed her attention.

She slipped out of the living room and into the kitchen, pausing at the rope covered scratching post her humans had conveniently installed in the pantry, and took a few seconds to hone her claws to needle like points. She would need them to be as sharp and deadly as possible.

She trotted over to the basement door and stood on her hind legs, her front paws twisting the knob and pulling the door open. Then she used her nose to push it open wide enough so that her slim body could slip through. She trotted down the stairs, turned right, and slipped through the crack behind the cask and into the darkness.

It didn't take long for her cat's eyes to become used to the absence of light and soon she could see just as good as any human with a flashlight. But she didn't really need her eyesight—she followed her instincts. Trotting down the twisting corridors, her calloused paws barely even registered the damp, coolness of the floor as she closed in on her quarry.

Less than a minute later, she saw the light, like a

beacon in the dark drawing her toward her destination. She picked up the pace, her paws silently slapping on the wet rock. She turned a corner and her whiskers tingled at the sight in front of her.

Sheriff Overton was hanging over a precipice, clutching on to a weathered plank, a flashlight sitting precariously on the edge next to him. She sniffed the air, her nose turning up at the foul stench of human fear.

She padded over to the board, sitting just on the very end and stared at him flicking her tail over the edge out into the precipice.

"Hi, kitty. Nice kitty." Overton's eyes were wide with fear as he looked from her to a rope that was tied to the wall.

"Get the rope." He nodded his head in the direction of the rope.

Belladonna made a big show of going over to the rope and rubbing against it. *Why not have some fun?*

"Yes. Good kitty." He crooned. "Bring it here and I'll give you a treat."

"Meow." Belladonna picked up the rope with her teeth and looked at him tentatively.

"Yes, that's right." He gestured with his hand for her to come toward him.

She took a few steps toward him, noting the hopeful look in his eye. She stared at him for a few heartbeats, then dropped the rope. His eyes turned cold and hard. She continued toward him, walking out onto the plank but staying far enough away so he couldn't grab her and send her over the edge. Her heartbeat drummed in her ears, her whiskers twitching with heightened awareness.

"Get the rope, you damn cat!" His voice was hard and rough.

Belladonna might have felt sorry for him if she didn't see the evil malice in his eyes. She thought back to all the things he'd done to her humans and her stomach curdled.

She inched closer, her highly developed senses knowing just how far away she should stay. Then, in a burst of energy, she shot out her paw, her claws shot out like switch blades and she raked them across the back of his hand.

"Ouch!" He jerked his hand away which also loosened his grip on the board. He dangled precariously by one hand, the other grappling for the board again. But Belladonna was too fast for him. Her paw shot out again, alternatively scratching his other hand and then slipping under the side of the board to pry his fingers.

She saw his hand loosen its grip. Overton was holding on only by the tips of his fingers now. She watched dispassionately as he flailed wildly trying to regain his grip on the board. She could have moved in for the kill and forced his fingers off, but she knew he wouldn't be able to support his weight for long.

She saw one finger slip off, then another and finally his whole hand slid off the board and into the darkness below.

"Nooooo!" His scream echoed in the passage. Then a loud splash.

She looked down into the hole ruefully. She took no pleasure in killing humans. Mice, on the other hand were a whole different story, she thought, eyeing a juicy brown field mouse as it scurried around a corner.

She tore her gaze away and leapt off the board to the safety of solid ground. She didn't have time to track down the mouse and besides, her humans never appreciated the warm, fur covered offerings of mice bodies she left for them after devouring the delicious heads.

She trotted off the way she had come, glancing back once over her shoulder at the gaping hole. She wondered if a human could survive the long fall and plunge into the icy ocean waters. Unlikely, she thought.

She didn't have much time to ponder it, though. She needed to get back to her humans. Her keen senses told her tonight would be extraordinary and they may need her services for even more important matters.

28

F *orty minutes until dead tide.*

LUKE SAT in the Bayliner cruiser, his binoculars in hand. The rocking motion of the boat did nothing to soothe his nerves—the tide was running out quickly now and so was his time. The bad guys would be here any minute.

Buzz turned on the motor and moved the boat forward a few feet. The pull of the tide was making it difficult for the anchor to keep the small boat in place.

Luke put the binoculars up to his face and continued his vigilant watch alternating his focus between the open ocean and the Blackmoore house.

He felt his shoulders knotting up with tension. He had no idea where these pirates were going to come from. His instincts told him they would come up the coast by boat, but he wasn't sure if they'd be coming from the north or the south. He'd positioned the boat in a spot where he could easily watch both sides.

But he couldn't take a risk they'd attack the Blackmoore house again, like they had during the summer, so he had men stationed all around the area ready to assist at the house or in the water at a moment's notice.

He scanned the yard with his binoculars, moving them slowly from the point of the cliff in the back to the front of the house, just to make sure no pirates were near the house. The girls were inside. His stomach clenched thinking about what happened during the summer—he'd never forgive himself if something happened to Morgan and he wasn't there to protect her.

Luke tapped the button on his communication set.

"Scott, do you see anything up by the house," he said into the mouthpiece clipped to his lapel.

"Not a peep." The voice came through his earpiece.

"Nothing out there, either," Buzz said from the front of the boat where he had his binoculars trained toward the open ocean. "You'd think they'd be here by now."

Luke nodded, a feeling of dread spreading inside

his chest. He pointed his binoculars at the cliff on the edge of the channel that led into Perkins Cove.

"The treasure could be right inside that channel," he said.

"Or over on the opposite side." Buzz pointed to the other side of the channel.

"Well, heck. I guess it could be anywhere," Luke said.

He studied the cliff with his binoculars. The hole from the explosion last summer stuck out like a sore thumb. Following the cliff line he noticed the opening at the mouth of the cave they'd explored on their dive the other day was sticking out above the water line. It was big enough to drive a small boat in.

Luke nudged Buzz with his elbow.

"Check out that cave we saw underwater the other day—you can almost drive a boat right into the opening."

Buzz aimed his binoculars in the direction Luke indicated. "Yeah. When the tide is fully out you *will* be able to drive a boat in there."

Luke saw a metallic reflection and his heart stopped. "What's that?"

"What?"

"I thought I saw something, over by the cave." He squinted into his binoculars, his nerves tense. And then he saw it again. A metal glint.

"I see it!" Buzz said.

Luke's heart sank when he realized what it was. A scuba diver ... and he was inflating a small boat complete with motor.

"It's the pirates!" Luke threw down his binoculars and ran to the wheel. "Pull up the anchor. They're scuba diving in ... and they have an inflatable. We need to follow them into the cave!"

Buzz ran over to the anchor pressing the switch for the motor. Luke tapped his fingers on the steering wheel cursing the anchor motor for its slowness. When he saw the anchor was almost up, he gunned the engine, taking the boat across the quarter mile of ocean as fast as it would go.

* * *

CELESTE LOOKED up from the reading the poetry book. Jolene seemed disinterested, but Morgan and Fiona had dreamy looks on their faces.

"Those poems are so romantic." Fiona sighed.

"Do you think that's why Isaiah picked this book as the cypher key?" Morgan asked.

"Maybe. Did you see the front of the book?" Fiona grabbed the book from Celeste and turned to the very first page. Inside was an inscription in pen.

To My Love MB From IB

"I BET Isaiah gave the book to his wife, Mariah," Morgan said.

"They must have had a great relationship," Celeste added. *Could she and Cal have the same kind of relationship? Or was it too late?*

Morgan tilted her head to the side and scrunched up her face. "Did you guys hear something?"

"No," they answered at the same time.

"What did you hear?" Fiona asked.

Morgan shook her head. "Oh, nothing."

But Celeste noticed she still had a strange look on her face.

"Meow." Belladonna announced her arrival and Celeste looked over at the cat.

"Oh, it was probably the cat you heard."

Belladonna jumped up on Celeste's lap and the smell of must tickled her nose. Celeste reached out to pet her and her fur was damp.

"Oh, Belladonna, you're all wet."

"And dirty," Jolene noted.

"Have you been in the basement catching mice again?" Fiona asked.

Belladonna answered them by curling into a ball in

Celeste lap, staring at them and blinking her eyes lazily before narrowing them into pre-slumber slits.

Fiona closed the poetry book and put it on the table. "It's so sweet how he gave her this book and carved their initials in the tree," she said referring to an old oak tree that towered over their shop *Sticks and Stones*. The land that the shop sat on had been in their family since Isaiah's time and someone had carved a heart with the initials IB and MB in it long ago. So long ago that the tree had grown and the initials were now twenty feet up. Naturally the girls assumed it was Isaiah and Mariah.

Earlier in the summer, they'd followed a trail of clues that they thought lead to a treasure. One of those clues was a note they found in a silver box they'd dug up.

YOU'LL FIND *the key you seek beneath the tree we vowed our love.*

THAT NOTE HAD LED them to the tree with the initials where they'd dug up a key that ended up being the key that opened the box the leather treasure map was in.

Celeste pressed her lips together. "It's almost as if Isaiah was leaving these clues *for* Mariah."

"That's what I was just thinking," Morgan said. "Remember the other clue about the key. That was written just for her because it said '*the tree we vowed our love*' and who else would know which tree that was besides Mariah?"

"He probably wanted her to be able to get to his treasure if something happened to him," Jolene added.

"I just wish he didn't have to be so cryptic about it." Celeste glanced at the clock, her stomach sinking. "It's almost dead tide and we still have no clue where the treasure is."

Jolene snapped her fingers. "Wait a minute!

The three sisters and Belladonna all swiveled their heads toward her.

"What?" Morgan asked.

Jolene stood and crossed over to the table that sat under the window. She reached into the long silver box that had held the leather map and pulled out the note they'd found in the lining.

"I think we might have interpreted this wrong." Jolene held the note up to face them.

Fiona scrunched up her face. "How so?"

"Well, see how it says *The Ocean's Revenge lies below my love?*" Jolene pointed to the second line in the poem.

"Yeah."

"We were interpreting that to mean it lies below the sea because the first line says *The sea is my love.*"

"Right." Morgan's eyebrows raised a fraction of an inch.

"Well, in the book he calls Mariah *my love*. What if the *my love* actually refers to Mariah and the poem means the *Ocean's Revenge* is below Mariah?"

"What would that mean? How could it be below her?" Fiona scrunched up her face at Jolene.

"Well it's kind of cryptic, but where would you find Mariah most of the time when she was alive?"

"Right here in the house he built for her," Morgan answered.

Celeste's heart skipped. It was all making sense now.

"Grandmas ghost told me not to take things too literally and *what we seek might be right underfoot*. At the time I thought she was just being vague, but what if she literally meant underfoot?"

"You mean under the house? But where? The basement is pretty much empty," Morgan said.

Celeste looked down at the floor. She remembered her trip to the basement and how the pirate ghost had been swirling around that big cask. Trying to pull her behind it. She shot out of her chair, causing Belladonna to fall to the floor with a thudding meow.

"There might be more to the basement then we realize. Follow me." Celeste turned toward the kitchen.

"Wait," Morgan said. She glanced down at the crystals that lay in the burlap sack at Fiona's feet. "Bring those, I have a feeling they might come in handy."

Fiona grabbed the sack then they all raced into the kitchen, hesitating only a second when they saw the basement door already open. Celeste flipped the switch for the basement light and took the stairs two at a time.

Stopping in front of the cask, she turned to face her sisters. "I heard Belladonna crying down here the other day and when I came down to rescue her I saw a ghost over here."

Jolene leaned over to inspect the side of the cask where Celeste was pointing.

"It seemed like he wanted me to go behind the cask," Celeste added.

"Maybe there is a passageway back there," Fiona said.

Celeste stared at Fiona's chest. The entire aquamarine pendant was glowing, a soft warm glow.

"What?" Fiona narrowed her eyes and looked at her other sisters who were also staring at her chest. "Why are you guys staring at me like that?"

Jolene pointed to the pendant "Your necklace. It's glowing."

"I thought I saw the bottom of it glowing upstairs, but figured it was just a trick of the light. But now … well it's clearly glowing," Morgan said, reaffirming what Celeste thought she had seen.

Fiona looked down. "Well that makes perfect sense. Aquamarine protects those who journey by sea. I bet the passage leads us down to the sea."

"Okay. So how do we get into this passage?" Jolene craned her neck around the cask, feeling the wall behind it.

"I have no idea." Celeste joined her and they pushed at the cask hoping to move it aside, but it wouldn't budge.

"Maybe there's an easier way." Morgan stepped to the front of the cask and put her palm on it. Closing her eyes she felt around the front, pressing and pushing. Then she smiled and nodded, her fingertips pressing in on a copper rivet.

With a click, the front of the cask swung open to reveal a passage. The girls slipped inside, the glow from Fiona's pendant lighting their way.

* * *

CAL DRUMMED his fingers impatiently against the counter at *Gino's Pizza* while he waited for his order.

"Large pepperoni?" The red aproned blonde smiled up at him from beneath her navy blue baseball cap.

Cal eyed the box suspiciously. He'd gotten the wrong pizza from *Gino's* more than once. He reached out to pry the top off. Except it wouldn't open. He took it in both hands and tried to force it, pinching at the corner on the bottom and pulling at the cover.

"Sorry, these covers can be a pain. It's almost like they're booby trapped or something," the girl said apologetically as she reached out to help him.

Booby trapped.

The word zinged in his mind and suddenly he knew the significance of the two maps. He grabbed his keys and ran for his car.

"Hey mister, don't you want your pizza?" the stunned girl at the counter yelled after him.

Cal broke all the speed limits on his way to the Blackmoore's. If the girls, Luke or Jake found out where the maze was and tried to go in without those two maps, the consequences could be deadly. The thought of something happening to any of them— especially Celeste—turned his insides cold.

He squealed to a stop in front of the house, ran up the steps and jerked the door open skidding his way down the hall and into the informal living room.

"I know what the two maps mean," he shouted to the empty room.

"Mew." Well, practically empty. Belladonna jumped down from the couch and walked over to the door leading to the kitchen.

"Hello! Celeste!" His heart sank when no one answered.

Where is everyone?

Cal glanced down at the table and saw the two maps were still there. He grabbed them and ran out into the hall checking all the rooms for the girls. They were nowhere to be found. His stomach clenched—had the pirates broken in and taken all four of them?

He checked the kitchen. The basement door stood open and the light was on. Belladonna sat in the doorway flicking her tail. *Had the girls gone in the basement for something?*

He ran down the stairs, Belladonna following at his heels. At the bottom of the steps, he looked to the left, his breath catching when he saw the cask with its false door hanging open.

He ran over to the cask and stuck his head in the door, the smell of salt air telling him immediately that he'd found the passage to the maze. The light from the basement illuminated the tunnel for a few feet, the rest was darkness except for the faint glow of a light up ahead. He patted his pocket, breathing a sigh of relief that he'd brought his small flashlight.

It was obvious the girls had either been taken in here by the pirates or come on their own. Either way, he needed to find them. He darted into the passage and sprinted in the direction of the faint glow.

29

*T*hirty minutes until dead tide.

LUKE HAD STOPPED the Bayliner just shy of the cave entrance—the tide wasn't low enough yet for the big boat to fit inside.

His fists clenched around the wheel, his knee jiggling up and down as he waited for Gordy to bring the inflatable—the only boat at his disposal that would allow them to follow the pirates into the cave. He couldn't wait for the tide to go out low enough to drive the Bayliner in and, besides, he had no idea how small the passages would be inside. He silently cursed himself for not anticipating the pirates might use scuba gear to sneak in underwater instead of arriving by boat. He hoped the mistake wouldn't prove to be fatal.

He cut the motor of the Bayliner and dropped anchor. He'd have to leave the boat here while he, Buzz and Gordy went in the raft. He double checked to make sure he had his Glock and SOG Seal knife.

"We should take this." Buzz held up the stainless steel scuba spear gun and Luke nodded. They could use all the weapons they could get.

The sound of a motor alerted him to the approaching inflatable and he sat on the side of the boat, swinging his legs over, so he could jump into the raft as soon as it came alongside.

Buzz did the same and when Gordy pulled up, they both jumped in causing the boat to dip into the water then bob back up.

"Let's go. They have a good five minutes on us," Luke said. Gordy gunned the boat forward and Luke picked up his infrared binoculars.

"It looks like they've moved the boulders that were blocking the way when we were in here the other day."

The missing boulders provided a small passageway for the craft and they slid through them followed the underwater passage for several yards. The water was getting much lower now and the passage much narrower. It was almost as if they were going uphill. Luke saw another passage to the right up ahead.

"Hold it up here," he said and Gordy stopped the boat. Luke looked down the other passage.

"Should we take it?" Gordy asked.

Luke got out a flashlight and put it down near the surface of the water, aiming it sideways so it would reflect off the top. He saw a slight rainbow sheen. Gasoline. The pirates must have taken that passage.

"Yep," he answered and Gordy turned the inflatable into the passage and headed forward.

As they powered along Luke kept his eye out on the sides of the tunnel in case there were any more turn offs.

"Buzz, keep an eye out up ahead. Let me know if you see any sign of the pirates. I'll keep an eye out for turnoffs ... I think we're in the maze and I have no idea which way to go.

* * *

"HOLY CRAP, we're inside the maze," Jolene said pointing to the carved stone walls which veered off at different angles.

"Wait." Celeste stopped short and spun around. "We need the map, or we won't know which path to take."

Jolene grabbed her arm, stopping her from heading back. "No we don't. I have a photographic memory, remember? I can picture the maze in my head and I know exactly which way to go."

Celeste's eyebrows raised. "Okay, then lead the way."

"Hold on," Morgan said. Celeste turned to see her looking down at the burlap bag Fiona was holding. Inside one of the crystals was glowing.

Fiona opened the bag and pulled out an egg sized pearly white stone which was emitting a hazy white glow, almost matching the one on her pendant.

"It's moonstone—for good fortune and safe travel." She held it out in her palm.

"Safe travel?" Celeste's brow creased. "Bring it over to the left path here."

Fiona moved to the left and the glow diminished, the further she walked down that path, the dimmer it got until finally the glow extinguished. She started back toward them and the stone lit up again, getting even brighter as she walked down the path on the right.

"Jolene, is that the path we should take?"

"Yep." Jolene nodded. "Looks like the stone is showing us the way, too."

They followed Fiona, getting about fifty feet down the path when Celeste thought she heard something behind them.

"Shhh." She grabbed Fiona's arm and they all stopped.

"Footsteps coming behind us," Morgan said.

Celeste instinctively got into her defensive karate stance, holding her arm with the cast in front of her, feeling glad she hadn't seen the doctor to have it removed. The hard shell of the cast would help protect her and she could use it as a weapon.

Was it the pirates coming after them?

The steps were closing in. She held her breath when she saw a shadowy figure turn the corner. Then her breath whooshed out of her and she relaxed when she realized who it was.

"Cal, you scared the crap out of us!"

Morgan bent down to pet Belladonna who purred up at her proudly as if expecting to be rewarded for bringing Cal.

"Thank God you guys are okay. I was afraid the pirates got you." Cal pulled Celeste into his arms and her heart melted. Then he abruptly released her and held the maps out in front of him, holding his flashlight in his mouth to illuminate them.

"I figured out how the maps work together," he said, except it came out all garbled around the flashlight.

"How?" Celeste asked, taking the flashlight out of his mouth and aiming it toward the maps.

"Remember how I told you that pirates used to set up booby traps to do away with other pirates that tried to steal their treasure?"

"Like the one that exploded the cliff when the pirates captured me this summer?" Morgan asked.

"Exactly," Cal said. "The map Jolene found shows you how to navigate the maze. But the maze is booby trapped. The leather map shows you where those booby traps are."

"That explains why the poem called it a *treacherous maze*," Morgan said.

Celeste frowned at the maps. "But how do you use them together?"

"That's the tricky part. You overlay them, but our maps aren't drawn to the same scale so you kind of have to wing it." Cal pointed to a round section in the middle of the leather map. "See this part?"

The girls nodded.

"Well it coincides with the very middle of the maze here." He pointed to an open space in the center of the maze. "So these X's on the leather map must be the booby trapped spots."

"There's a lot of them in the middle." Celeste noticed.

"Right, I think that's where the treasure is so it makes sense he'd have them there. But there's also some spots out here in the maze so we need to be on the lookout for those and make sure we avoid them … whatever they are."

Cal narrowed his eyes at Fiona, apparently noticing the moonstone for the first time. "What's going on with that rock?"

"It's showing us the way. Lights up when we are heading in the right direction, then fades if we make a wrong turn."

Cal's eyebrows raised a fraction of an inch.

"Well, that's handy," he said matter-of-factly. Celeste figured he must be getting used to the sister's strange powers.

"So anyway," he said, turning back to the maps and pointing to one section. "It looks like we are here on the maze map. If we follow the maze as the map indicates, I think we'll need to be careful here … and here. The rest of the booby traps look like they are at the destination."

"What *is* the destination?" Jolene asked.

"I don't know, but it looks like it must be huge," Celeste replied.

"I assumed it was the treasure," Morgan added.

"Well, heck, then lets get going," Jolene said turning and starting to walk in the direction they had been going. "We may still be able to beat the pirates there before they realize they have the wrong map and figure out the way to the treasure."

They continued through the maze, the moonstone and Jolene's memory showing them the way. Celeste turned off the flashlight to conserve the battery just in case. As they progressed Celeste could feel it get damper, cooler and saltier. They were nearing the ocean.

"Hold on." Cal held the maps out and Celeste clicked on the flashlight and aimed it at them.

"If my theory is correct, there's a booby trap up here to the left—we better be careful."

They all scooted to the right of the passage and Celeste pointed the flashlight to the left side. She noticed even Belladonna was keeping to the right. The flashlight hit on a sandy patch of floor.

"There!" Cal said.

"The sand?" Jolene asked.

"Don't step near it." Cal picked up a stick that was lying on the side and poked it in the sand. It went in about a foot, then stood straight up and slowly sunk.

"Quicksand!"

Celeste's stomach crunched thinking of what might have happened to them if Cal hadn't figured out the two maps. The area of sand looked just like any other patch of sand and the passage was loaded with it. They could have walked right over it.

They shuffled by it, each of them giving the area a wide berth. Belladonna trotted by with a quiet "mew".

A few more twists and turns and Cal raised the alarm again. "Watch out up ahead on the right."

They cautiously approached, Celeste's heart skittering when the flashlight revealed old rusted animal traps set along the path. Easy to pick out with the flashlight, but for a pirate trying to navigate the dark passage in the 1700s not so much. She looked nervously for Belladonna but she needn't have worried, the cat was staying far away from them.

They carefully set the traps to the side and continued on their way. After a few more minutes the passage seemed to get wider and wider until they spilled out into a gigantic cavern. Fiona's crystal glowed like someone had plugged it in, illuminating the entire chamber.

Celeste's heart forgot to beat as she looked around the chamber. Her mouth dropped open and she glanced sideways at her sisters, each of whom wore expressions similar to hers.

For once, the Blackmoore sisters were all speechless.

30

D *ead Tide*

"Is that what I think it is?" Jolene asked, her eyes staring straight ahead.

"Yep." Celeste gulped.

The passage had opened up to a giant cavern ... a cavern big enough to hold a three hundred year old pirate galleon. Which it did.

"*The Ocean's Revenge*—Isaiah Blackmoore's ship." Jolene pointed to the ship's name burned into the wood on the front and Celeste felt an odd mixture of wonder and pride swell in her chest.

The path had spilled them out just above the ships

deck. Below them, Celeste could see the bottom of the cavern was filled with about twenty feet of seawater that was rushing out rapidly. When dead tide hit, the bottom would be dry offering easy access to the hold of the ship. And, if what she could see on the deck of the ship was any indication, the whole thing was loaded with treasure.

Looking across the cavern, she could see openings from other passageways. One was almost directly across from them. Another was to the right and one level below. Celeste realized the maze must have more than one level.

The ship was intact, almost perfectly preserved if not a little weathered from the centuries of being underwater.

Jolene started off down the rocky slope that led to the ship, but Cal pulled her back.

"Hold on. This place is booby trapped, remember?" He held out the two maps. "Let's figure out where the traps are and then we can check out the ship."

Celeste walked around to the other side of the maps, orienting herself so that the maps faced the same way as the cavern. "This 'X', right here, looks like it's right in front of the ship … at the bow."

Cal looked over at the ship. "You're right. There's water there now but we better be careful not to step there once it's out … no telling what Isaiah put there."

"And over here to the right." Morgan pointed to an area of rock.

"Yes, and it looks like there is something over there … and there." Cal pointed to spots on the map that looked like they were on either side of the ship, near the passage openings.

"And what ever you do, don't go near there." Cal pointed his chin to the right where there was a tall outcropping of rock.

"Why?" Jolene asked.

Celeste stood on her tip-toes to get a better look. "Is that an underground cliff?"

"Yep," Cal said. "And from the looks of it, it's pretty deep. You don't want to fall over that by mistake."

Jolene shook her head, and then returned to looking at the maps. "That looks like all of the booby traps, right?"

Cal nodded. "Near as I can tell."

"Good. Then let's check it out." Jolene picked her way down the steep rubble trail and everyone followed. The floor on this side of the cavern was higher than the rest and a wooden plank spanned the space from one section of the trail to the deck of the ship. They crossed the plank, Celeste's stomach lurching as she looked at the icy water swirling below. The current was strong—if one of them fell in, they might be sucked out to sea.

"This is amazing." Morgan stood on the deck, looking up at the tall mast of the ship. She touched the age old wood, closing her eyes and smiling. Celeste thought she saw a swirly mist start to form next to Morgan but when she blinked it was gone.

"I can't believe this thing has survived almost intact down here all these years." Celeste looked around at the wooden deck, brass ships wheel and hand carved ornamentation near the front of the ship. She felt like she had been transported into the middle of an *Indiana Jones* movie.

Jolene was already across the deck and into the opening to the ship's hold, which was practically glowing with gold and silver.

"Look at this!" She held up a giant gold cross embedded with emerald green stones that glinted in the light. Celeste watched her run her fingers through the booty that was piled up inside the ship and realized it was loaded with jewelry, coins and artifacts worth more money than they could ever spend.

Looking around she could see some of the treasure was strewn about the cavern which also held old casks and wooden sea chests.

She squatted down beside Jolene and stared at the treasure. "How are we going to get this stuff out of here?"

"You won't need to worry about that." Celeste

jerked her head in the direction of the voice, her heart-beat pounding in her chest as she recognized the pirates from Skinner's house. They were standing in the opening of one of the passages across the cavern and to the right. One of them still had the jagged scar on the side of his face. The other wore a "pirate-style" black eye patch held across the eye that had been skewered by the shard from Fiona's necklace.

She stood frozen, staring at the pirates, wondering how they had found their way here with the wrong map.

Jolene stood up, facing them with her hands on her hip. "This treasure is ours … back off!"

"I don't think so Missy." Scarface raised his gun pointing it directly at Jolene who barely even flinched. Celeste could see her sister's fists clenching and unclenching. She remembered the lightning-like energy she'd branded Scarface with.

"Wait, you idiot." Eye Patch put his palm on the top of the barrel of Scarface's gun. "You can't shoot that in here, it could bring the whole cavern down on top of us."

Scarface looked disappointed, Jolene looked triumphant.

"We'll just have to take them the old fashioned way then," Scarface growled. Celeste's stomach sank as four more pirates appeared behind him and they started across the cavern toward them.

"Hold it right there!" The voice came from the left, a level higher than where Celeste was now. She swiveled her head in that direction and relief swept over her when she saw Luke, Buzz and Gordy.

Unfortunately, Luke had captured the pirates' attention too.

Eye Patch yelled, "Get them!" and changed course rushing up the boulders on the side of the cavern to get to the flat mouth of the passage that Luke was standing in. They split up with two of the new pirates following Eye Patch and the other two following Scarface who kept coming toward Jolene and Celeste.

Celeste watched helplessly as the three pirates rushed Luke, Buzz and Gordy. Eyepatch brandished a large oar trying to jab and hit Luke. Luke had a knife out, but Eyepatch was keeping him from getting near with the long oar. The other two had engaged Buzz and Gordy in a fist fight and the four of them were rolling around in the debris below the passage. It was impossible to tell who was winning.

Celeste noticed the water was receding quickly. Scarface and his friends were sloshing their way toward the ship, the water now only waist deep.

Over on the left, Luke was dodging Eye Patch's oar, unsuccessfully trying to grab for it. Celeste saw a white mist materialize behind him. She squinted at it—it was the pirate ghost! The ghost was gesturing wildly at an old sea chest that sat just behind Luke.

Was there something in there that could help them?

"Luke," she yelled across the cavern, pointing at the chest. "The chest! Look in the chest!"

Luke risked a glance behind him and then pushed hard at Eye Patch, who lost his balance and fell back a few steps. Luke backed up, his attention still focused on Eye Patch, and flipped open the lid of the chest. Celeste saw his eyes widen as he quickly glanced back over his shoulder to look inside. Then he reached into the chest and came out with a long sword.

Celeste watched in astonishment as he proceeded to wield the sword against Eye Patch's oar in a choreography that was reminiscent of an old-fashioned sword fight. Out of the corner of her eye, she saw one of the other pirates land a punishing blow to Gordy who collapsed in a heap.

She didn't have much time to feel bad for him though because Scarface and the two other pirates were getting close to the ship. Too close. She remembered the booby trap directly in front of the galleon.

Could she lure them over there?

Celeste ran to the front of the ship, a wooden plank hung out over the bow like a gangplank and she jumped on top of it, ignoring her sister's pleas for her to stop.

"You'll never take us or our treasure!" she yelled, glaring down at Scarface and his companions.

"Argghh!" One of them surged forward toward the front of the ship where she leaned over teasingly. The ship was a good twenty feet above the ground, and the fastest route to her was to climb a rope that was dangling over the front. The pirate saw the rope and ran forward to grab it, stepping directly in front of the ship, but instead of his feet hitting the solid ground of the cavern floor, he slid into the swirling water. From her vantage point above on the ship, Celeste noticed it was swirling around in a circle—a whirlpool.

The pirate screamed and flailed his arms up in the air. His body spun in the current as it disappeared quickly under the water.

Scarface and the other pirate stopped in their tracks, watching as their cohort was sucked under, into the icy dark water. They quickly changed direction, heading to the side of the ship. Celeste noticed with a tinge of panic that, other than the whirlpool, only a trickle of water was left on the bottom of the cavern. It was dead tide and soon the tide would start rushing in again. If they didn't hurry, they'd all be trapped in here with all the exits under water.

Celeste stole a glance over at Gordy. He lay still on

the rocks. The pirate who had knocked him out was making his way up to join Eye Patch in the sword fight. Buzz was holding his ground against the other pirate.

"Luke!" Cal caught Luke's attention, and pointed to Luke's right. Celeste knew he was trying to tell Luke a booby trap lay there, but would Luke know what he meant?

Celeste ran off the ship and onto a large boulder so she could get a better look. She held her breath as Luke backed the pirates up, advancing slowly as he jabbed at them with the sword. His sword ripped the sleeve of Eye Patch and Celeste saw a line of blood.

"Bastard!" Eye Patch paused to look at his arm which was a fatal mistake. Luke took the opportunity to ram the sword into his midsection, causing Eye Patch to stumble back into the other pirate. They both staggered backward a couple of feet, stopping abruptly as if stuck in mud. Celeste looked down at their feet … not mud … quicksand.

They were wide eyed with panic as their attempts to pull their feet out only served to get them sucked in deeper. She watched them struggle as they sunk to their ankles. Then their knees. Then their waist.

"Help us!" Eye Patch pleaded, holding his arms out to Luke. But Luke was already rushing over to the passage opening he'd come in through. Celeste saw him pick up a spear gun and aim it in the direction of Buzz and the pirate he was still trying to fight off.

He shot it and the spear flew out.

"Ahhhh!" The pirate whipped around, grabbing for the spear as it connected with his shoulder blade. That gave Buzz the opening he needed to knock the pirate out cold, and then he headed in the direction of Gordy, presumably to pull him out of the way of the raising water.

Celeste didn't have time to watch Gordy's rescue though because she was too busy watching Scarface's ugly mug appear over the side of the ship.

"Look out!" She yelled to Jolene, who was still standing on the deck with Fiona.

Below Fiona the burlap bag glowed red. Belladonna sat beside the bag, pawing at it and meowing.

"The bag!" Celeste pointed to the bag as Scarface pushed himself up onto the end of the plank that hung over the front of the ship, a triumphant snarl on his face.

Jolene bent down, opened the bag and took out the glowing crystal. The crystal brightened when she touched it arcing out energy in vibrant reds and oranges.

Scarface lunged toward Jolene.

Jolene hurled the crystal at him, sparks flying out of her hand as the glowing ball left it.

Scarface stopped short, realizing the ball was coming straight for him. He tried to back up the plank, but the ball exploded in front of him knocking him off the ship. Celeste heard his yell and then the splash as he was swallowed by the whirlpool.

Sparks from the crystal rained down on the ship like fireworks. No one spoke. What was there to say?

Celeste saw Buzz and Luke wading through the water with Gordy's body. She hoped he wasn't dead.

Had they killed all the pirates?

Celeste did a mental headcount … there was one pirate left. She scanned the cavern. Where was he?

She got her answer seconds later when she felt strong hands grabbed her around the waist and the cold steel of a blade press against her throat.

"Get away from the treasure or I'll kill her." Celeste's heart pounded against her ribs as the gravely voice yelled against her ear.

She saw the alarm in her sister's eyes as they turned toward her. Jolene glanced down at the crystals. None of them glowed.

"Let her go!" Jolene pushed her palm out toward the pirate but nothing happened.

Fiona started toward them and the pirate jerked on Celeste's hair, pulling her head to the side and jabbing the pointy edge of the blade into her neck, just under her chin. Celeste flinched and Fiona stopped.

"What do you want?" Morgan asked.

"All the treasure I can carry and safe passage out of here the way you came in." The pirate jerked his head toward the passage the girls had arrived through. Celeste cut her eyes toward the other side, where the pirates had come and noticed it was already starting to fill with water. His exit route was probably cut off.

She also saw Cal creeping toward them and she tried to signal to him to back off. She had a plan and didn't want Cal getting hurt.

"Okay, but let her go first," Morgan said.

Celeste stayed very still, keeping in tune with the pirates every breath, waiting for him to loosen his hold just a little.

A white blur streaked from the side, distracting the pirate.

Belladonna!

The cat raked the pirates arm with her claws.

The pirate loosened his grip and Celeste spun around, bringing her arm up and smashed him over the head as hard as she could with her hard plaster cast.

He staggered backward and Cal moved in, hitting him with an uppercut to the jaw. But the pirate was tough and he punched out connecting with Cal's cheek. Cal punched back, moving the pirate back a few steps.

The pirate swung again and Cal ducked low then rushed into the pirate's midsection pushing him backward like a linebacker. Celeste's stomach clenched when she realized what Cal was doing—he was pushing the pirate toward the cliff and at the speed he was going, it looked like Cal was going to go right over with him.

"Cal, no!" She cried out just as he disappeared over the edge.

* * *

CELESTE RUSHED to the edge of the cliff, her heart shattering into a million pieces. Tears sprang to her eyes as she peered over and got the surprise of her life. Cal wasn't crushed at the bottom … actually, you couldn't even see the bottom but that was okay because Cal's hand was gripping onto a piece of rock that was sticking out about six inches down.

"Cal! I thought you were dead."

"Yeah, me too." He grinned up at her.

"Grab onto my hand with your free hand." She shoved her good hand, the one without the cast, over the cliff. He grabbed it. His hand was slick with sweat and her heart fluttered half expecting it to slip out. In that moment, she knew that she didn't want to live without him.

"Cal, I love you," she blurted out.

His blue eyes softened and he smiled up at her. "I love you, too, Celeste."

They stared into each other's eyes. Celeste could feel his heart beating through her hand. Her chest filled with warmth, and then panic as she felt his hand slipping out of hers.

"No!" she yelled as she tried to grab on, but his hand was too slick, his body weight too heavy. His hand slipped out of hers and she closed her eyes, waiting to hear the sickening crunch.

No crunch came.

She opened her eyes and craned her neck further over the edge. Cal was standing on a thin ledge, pressed against the wall of the cliff, his face about a foot down looking up at her.

"You didn't fall to your death!"

"Nah, I was standing on the ledge the whole time. Now hurry up and help me out of here."

She lay down on her stomach and put both hands over. Cal grabbed on then wedged his foot into a crevice on the side of the cliff pulling his way up like a mountain climber.

They were both out of breath when he emerged over the top. He pulled her to her feet and pushed the hair back from her face.

"Did you mean what you said?" he asked.

"What? That I love you?"

He nodded, his sapphire eyes drilling into hers.

"Well, after that stunt, I'm not so sure," she teased. Out of the corner of her eye she could see her pirate ghost bobbing up and down, smiling and giving her the thumbs up.

"Say it," he said, his lips drifting awfully close to hers.

"I love you." His lips were warm, salty and utterly delicious. As her eyes fluttered shut, she saw the pirate ghost blow her a kiss and disappear into a swirl of mist.

"Hey, you guys hurry up! The tide is coming in!" Morgan's frantic plea jerked Celeste out of the kiss and she looked around.

How had the water gotten so high so fast?

She grabbed Cal's hand and sprinted over to where her sisters stood gesturing for them to hurry. Luke and Buzz stood with Gordy in between them, a little bruised but alive.

"We'll have to go out this way." Luke nodded toward the passage the girls had used. "The way we came is already getting flooded and I'm not sure we can fit the boat through."

Celeste looked over to the other side of the cavern and noticed the water was a lot higher on that side. She glanced at the *Ocean's Revenge* and saw the boat was quickly filling up with water.

"But what about the treasure?" she asked.

"There's no time. Let's go!"

They ran up the slope and into the passage. Fiona held her crystal out which lit the way. Buzz and Gordy raised their brows at it but kept quiet.

Celeste noticed, the bottom of the passage was slick with puddles of water as they hurried through it, her heart warmed by the fact that Cal kept hold of her hand. Belladonna padded along behind them making angry mewing noises every time her paws got wet.

"So how do you guys figure the pirates knew their way through the maze?" Jolene asked.

"We followed them in from the ocean," Luke said. "I found this in the water floating behind them. I guess they used it to find their way. Very convenient they dropped it since it helped us find *our* way."

He pulled out a map almost identical to the maze map they had.

"Let me see that." Jolene stopped and stared at the map. "This isn't the fake that we gave to Overton."

"What? It has to be," Morgan said.

"No. The path is actually the real path—the opposite of the fake map." Jolene turned to Cal. "Do you still have that?"

Cal reached into his pocket and pulled out the map. Jolene held the two side by side.

"See."

"How is that possible?" Fiona made a face. "What is going on?"

"There's only one way it's possible." Jolene chuckled. "Overton was double-crossing Goldlinger."

"Right!" Celeste said. "He took our fake map and made his own fake map which actually had the real path!"

Morgan's brow creased. "But what happened to Overton."

Jolene shrugged. "Who knows. Who cares."

"Maybe Goldlinger found out and did away with him?" Fiona mused.

"Mew!"

"Belladonna sounds like maybe she knows," Celeste joked.

"This is kind of depressing. We went to all this trouble … found the treasure, fought off the pirates and we didn't even get to bring any of the treasure back!" Fiona said.

"Speak for yourself." Jolene reached into the pocket of her cargo pants and pulled out a handful of gold chains and coins.

"You took some?" Morgan asked as they rounded the last corner. The basement light shone through the cask door just ahead.

"Yeah, what do you think I was doing while you guys were screwing off with the pirates?"

Belladonna ran ahead, leaping out into the basement and up the steps. The rest of them dragged behind. Celeste felt exhausted as they mounted the stairs and spilled out into the kitchen.

Jake came around the corner, creasing his forehead at them. "Where *were* you guys. I looked all over."

They looked at each other. No one knew exactly what to say.

Jake narrowed his eyes. "Did I miss something? It's past midnight and I thought that was when everything was going to go down."

Fiona went over to him and put her arm around his waist. "You could say that."

Jake slipped his arm around her shoulders and looked at the basement door. "Were you guys in the basement?"

"Yes. I don't know about anyone else, but *I* worked up quite an appetite down there," Jolene said. "Let's fill Jake in while we eat that pizza."

Celeste felt Cal cringe as Jolene glanced at the kitchen counters then poked her head into the informal living room, then back into the kitchen.

"Cal, don't tell me you forgot to pick up the pizza?"

EPILOGUE

"It's nice to sit and relax without having to worry about pirates." Jolene lifted her face to the sun, whose warm Indian summer rays had transformed the Maine fall weather back into summer.

Celeste nodded, looking out over Perkins Cove where they sat at wrought iron tables outside their favorite ice cream place. The cove was calm, peaceful. A perfect fall day which had tourists swarming in and out of the shops and taking pictures of themselves in front of the cove filled with quaint New England boats. She felt the corners of her mouth tug upwards in a smile thinking of how surprised they might be to know a three hundred year old pirate ship loaded with treasure was less than a mile away.

"You can say that again," Cal said pulling out the

chair next to Celeste and setting a small cup of chocolate chip ice cream in front of her before sitting down.

Celeste dug into the ice cream, which was no easy feat considering Cal had intertwined his hand with hers and didn't seem eager to let go. Luckily her cast had been removed a week ago and she had more mobility in her free hand.

"I just wish we had taken more treasure out. It could be another three hundred years before anyone can get down there again." Morgan bit into the side of her maple walnut cone with a crunch.

"Not necessarily," Jake said. "Back in Isaiah's day there wouldn't have been anyway to navigate the maze under water, but today we have scuba gear and even submersibles that could go down there."

"I'd love to get a look at what's in there," Cal said. "There must be some great antique jewelry and artifacts. Priceless stuff. But really, the things you guys have in your attic will give you more money than you can ever spend."

"I still don't understand how Isaiah got the boat in there in the first place," Fiona said.

"When we were out on the ocean looking for the pirates, I could see the opening of the underwater cave above the sea line. I'm guessing he just sailed the boat in. Three hundred years ago the sea level was actually a lot lower, so if they had an unusually low tide like this one, he would have been able to get the boat in pretty easily," Jake said.

"But how would he get it through the maze?" Jolene sipped her frappe, her blue eyes questioning Jake over the tops of her sunglasses.

"I think he might have built the maze later as added insurance against anyone else finding the ship."

Celeste's eyebrows shot up. "That seems like a pretty big task."

Jake shrugged. "Well I'm not sure how he did it, but somehow he got that boat in there in the middle of the maze."

"And what about Overton?" Cal asked.

"No one has seen him since last week," Jake answered.

Celeste licked a glob of ice cream off her spoon. It had been a little over a week since they'd found the pirate ship and no one had seen Overton since that day. She couldn't say she would miss him, but it did give her an eerie feeling not knowing what happened to him.

"Well, I hope they get a nicer Sheriff to replace him. It will be great not to be accused of every crime that happens in this town," Morgan said shoving the end of her cone into her mouth.

"Do you think Goldlinger did away with him?" Jolene asked.

Jake shrugged. "I'm not sure. His apartment was empty and no one ever found his car. Maybe he's on the run."

"Either way, I'm happy to see him go."

"So now what?" Fiona asked. "We go back to normal?"

"Well, I'd hardly call you girls *normal*," Cal said draping his arm over Celeste's chair.

"Right. We have some special talents that we can't ignore," Celeste said as she squinted at the crowd. *Was that who she thought it was?*

"Yeah, we should work on harnessing them, I guess," Fiona said, "especially Jolene."

"I don't even know where to start," Jolene said. "Maybe you could help me, Celeste."

"Yeah, sure," Celeste answered her sister absently. She was distracted by the crowd, her eyes searching for a mop of familiar dark, wavy hair she *thought* she'd seen.

"Maybe we could all get together once a week or something and ... Celeste ... Are you even listening?" Jolene tapped Celeste on the shoulder.

Celeste wasn't listening. She was busy staring into the crowd ... at Mateo. He stood about fifty feet away on the other side of the cove watching them. When he saw her look at him, he smiled, saluted her and then turned away, disappearing into a throng of tourists who'd just disembarked from one of the open air trolley shaped buses that provided transportation around town.

"Hey, it's that guy!" Jolene, who had swiveled her head to follow Celeste's gaze shot out of her chair and took off running in Mateo's direction. Celeste relaxed back in her seat. Somehow she knew Jolene would never catch up to him.

"What guy?" Fiona scrunched her face at Celeste.

"Mateo."

"Oh, the mystery man who gave us the book." Fiona looked in the direction Jolene had taken off in. "Why do you think he would show up here? Should we go after him?"

Celeste shrugged. "Nah. He helped us out before, but if he wanted to talk to us he would have come over."

"Besides," Morgan added. "I have a feeling we might be seeing him again someday … when the time is right."

Celeste watched Jolene come out of the crowd and jog back to the table.

"He got away." She collapsed in her seat, gulping in a few breaths.

"Never mind him," Morgan said. "Luke called me last night and he said his boss was asking a lot of questions about our ... umm ... unusual talents. I guess word travels fast."

"I think I'd feel better if less people knew about that." Celeste cut her eyes over to Morgan.

"Me too. But they found out somehow and were intrigued."

"Speak of the devil." Jolene lifted her chin toward the street and Celeste looked over her shoulder to see Luke approaching the table. He pulled a chair over next to Morgan and everyone at the table exchanged a round of greetings.

"How was your trip?" Cal asked.

"Pretty good. How have things been here?"

"Blissfully quiet," Celeste answered.

"Almost too quiet," Jolene said. "It's getting kind of boring."

"Oh really?" Luke leaned back in his chair crossing his arms against his chest and smiling. "So you girls are looking to spice things up?"

Celeste narrowed her eyes. *Was she?* The truth was after all the excitement it *was* getting kind of boring. Maybe she was getting addicted to danger. She looked around at her sisters and got the distinct impression they felt the same way.

Jolene answered for all of them. "Yes, we are."

"Great." Luke leaned his forearms on the table, his eyes sparkling. "How do you guys feel about ghost towns in the old west? I have a job out there and I sure could use your help.

THE END.

* * *

SIGN UP below for an exclusive never-before-published novella from my Lexy Baker culinary mystery series plus you'll be added to my VIP reader list to get all my latest releases at the lowest discount price:

http://www.leighanndobbs.com/newsletter

IF YOU WANT to receive a text message alert on your cell phone for new releases , text COZYMYSTERY to 88202 (sorry, this only works for US cell phones!)

CONNECT ON FACEBOOK - Join my private readers group on Facebook and get a sneak peek at what I'm working on plus connect with like-minded readers and discuss our favorite books:

https://www.facebook.com/groups/ldobbsreaders

Want more Blackmoore Sister's adventures? Buy the rest of the books in the series:

Dead Wrong

Dead & Buried

Dead Tide

Buried Secrets

Deadly Intentions

A Grave Mistake

Spell Found

Fatal Fortune

Mooseamuck Island Cozy Mystery Series

* * *

A Zen For Murder

A Crabby Killer

A Treacherous Treasure

Mystic Notch

Cat Cozy Mystery Series

* * *

Ghostly Paws

A Spirited Tail

A Mew To A Kill

Paws and Effect

Probable Paws

Blackmoore Sisters

Cozy Mystery Series

* * *

Dead Wrong

Dead & Buried

Dead Tide

Buried Secrets

Deadly Intentions

A Grave Mistake

Spell Found

Fatal Fortune

Lexy Baker Cozy Mystery Series

* * *

Lexy Baker Cozy Mystery Series Boxed Set Vol 1 (Books 1-4)

Or buy the books separately:

Killer Cupcakes

Dying For Danish

Murder, Money and Marzipan

3 Bodies and a Biscotti

Brownies, Bodies & Bad Guys

Bake, Battle & Roll

Wedded Blintz

Scones, Skulls & Scams

Ice Cream Murder

Mummified Meringues

Brutal Brulee (Novella)

No Scone Unturned

Cream Puff Killer

Hazel Martin Historical Mystery Series

***

Murder at Lowry House (book 1)

Murder by Misunderstanding (book 2)

Lady Katherine Regency Mysteries

***

An Invitation to Murder (Book 1)

The Baffling Burglaries of Bath (Book 2)

Sam Mason Mysteries

(As L. A. Dobbs)

***

Telling Lies (Book 1)

Keeping Secrets (Book 2)

Exposing Truths (Book 3)

Betraying Trust (Book 4)

Romantic Comedy

***

Corporate Chaos Series

In Over Her Head (book 1)

Can't Stand the Heat (book 2)

What Goes Around Comes Around (book 3)

Contemporary Romance

***

Reluctant Romance

Sweet Romance (Written As Annie Dobbs)

Firefly Inn Series

***

Another Chance (Book 1)

Another Wish (Book 2)

Hometown Hearts Series

***

No Getting Over You (Book 1)

A Change of Heart (Book 2)

***

Sweetrock Sweet and Spicy Cowboy Romance

Some Like It Hot

Too Close For Comfort

——

Regency Romance

* * *

Scandals and Spies Series:

Kissing The Enemy

Deceiving the Duke

Tempting the Rival

Charming the Spy

Pursuing the Traitor

Captivating the Captain

The Unexpected Series:

An Unexpected Proposal

An Unexpected Passion

Dobbs Fancytales:

Dobbs Fancytales Boxed Set Collection

———

Western Historical Romance

***

Goldwater Creek Mail Order Brides:

Faith

American Mail Order Brides Series:

Chevonne: Bride of Oklahoma

————————

Magical Romance with a Touch of Mystery

***

Something Magical

Curiously Enchanted

ROMANTIC SUSPENSE

WRITING AS LEE ANNE JONES:

***

The Rockford Security Series:

NOTE FROM THE AUTHOR

I hope you enjoyed reading this book as much as I enjoyed writing it. This is the third book in the Blackmoore sisters mystery series and I have a whole bunch more planned!

The setting for this book series is based on one of my favorite places in the world - Ogunquit Maine. Of course, I changed some of the geography around to suit my story, and changed the name of the town to Noquitt but the basics are there. Anyone familiar with Ogunquit will recognize some of the landmarks I have in the book.

The house the sisters live in sits at the very end of Perkins Cove and I was always fascinated with it as a kid. Of course, back then it was a mysterious, creepy old house that was privately owned and I was dying to go in there. I'm sure it must have had an attic stuffed full of antiques just like in the book!

Today, it's been all modernized and updated—I think you can even rent it out for a summer vacation. In the book the house looks different and it's also set high up on a cliff (you'll see why in a later book) where in real life it's not. I've also made the house much older to suit my story.

Believe it or not, much of the pirate lore I have in the book is actually true! Pirates really did bury treasure all along the east coast and there was a stash of pirate booty dug up in the 1930s in Biddeford like I mention in the book.

This book has been through many edits with several people and even some software programs, but since nothing is infallible (even the software programs) you might catch a spelling error or mistake and, if you do, I sure would appreciate it if you let me know - you can contact me at lee@leighanndobbs.com.

Oh, and I love to connect with my readers so please do visit me on facebook at http://www.facebook.com/leighanndobbsbooks or at my website http://www.leighanndobbs.com.

Want a free never-before-published novella from my Lexy Baker culinary mystery series? Go to:

http://www.leighanndobbs.com/newsletter and enter your email address to signup - I promise never to share it and I only send emails every couple of weeks so I won't fill up your inbox.

ABOUT THE AUTHOR

USA Today Bestselling author Leighann Dobbs has had a passion for reading since she was old enough to hold a book, but she didn't put pen to paper until much later in life. After a twenty-year career as a software engineer with a few side trips into selling antiques and making jewelry, she realized you can't make a living reading books, so she tried her hand at writing them and discovered she had a passion for that, too! She lives in New Hampshire with her husband, Bruce, their trusty Chihuahua mix, Mojo, and beautiful rescue cat, Kitty.

Sign up below for an exclusive never-before-published novella from her Lexy Baker culinary mystery series plus you'll be added to my VIP reader list to get all her latest releases at the lowest discount price:

http://www.leighanndobbs.com/newsletter

If you want to receive a text message alert on your cell phone for new releases , text COZYMYSTERY to 88202 (sorry, this only works for US cell phones!)

Connect with Leighann on Facebook:

http://facebook.com/leighanndobbsbooks

This is a work of fiction.

None of it is real. All names, places, and events are products of the author's imagination. Any resemblance to real names, places, or events are purely coincidental, and should not be construed as being real.

Made in the USA
Middletown, DE
26 August 2018